"Do I make myself clear?" Matt asked.

"I want no fe... That's it."

"Certainly, si... aplomb. "Yo... ...empered at all times, no matter what the provocation."

He grimaced. "No, that's not what I mean. I am not unreasonable. But if you start this maudlin business of fancying yourself in love with me, you're out, Carmody. I will not be subjected to that again."

Ann quickly swallowed an urge to laugh at his outrageous arrogance. "I see no difficulty there, sir."

"Good," he said. "I've been so provoked by this idiotic situation I was tempted to hire a man this time."

Ann stared back at him, poker-faced. "I'm sure I won't trouble you, sir. Actually, I prefer younger men."

Emma Darcy nearly became an actress until her fiancé declared he preferred to attend the theater *with* her. She became a wife and mother. Later she took up oil painting—unsuccessfully, she remarks. Then, she tried architecture, designing the family home in New South Wales. Next came romance writing—''the hardest and most challenging of all the activities,'' she confesses.

Books by Emma Darcy

HARLEQUIN ROMANCE
2900—BLIND DATE
2941—WHIRLPOOL OF PASSION

HARLEQUIN PRESENTS
1020—THE WRONG MIRROR
1033—THE ONE THAT GOT AWAY
1048—STRIKE AT THE HEART
1080—THE POSITIVE APPROACH
1103—MISTRESS OF PILLATORO
1151—ALWAYS LOVE
1177—A PRICELESS LOVE
1199—THE ALOHA BRIDE
1232—THE FALCON'S MISTRESS
1272—THE POWER AND THE PASSION
1288—THE ULTIMATE CHOICE

Don't miss any of our special offers. Write to us at the following address for information on our newest releases.

Harlequin Reader Service
901 Fuhrmann Blvd., P.O. Box 1397, Buffalo, NY 14240
Canadian address: P.O. Box 603,
Fort Erie, Ont. L2A 5X3

PATTERN OF DECEIT

Emma Darcy

Harlequin Books

TORONTO • NEW YORK • LONDON
AMSTERDAM • PARIS • SYDNEY • HAMBURG
STOCKHOLM • ATHENS • TOKYO • MILAN

Original hardcover edition published in 1989
by Mills & Boon Limited

ISBN 0-373-03085-1

Harlequin Romance first edition November 1990

Copyright © 1989 by Emma Darcy.
All rights reserved. Except for use in any review, the reproduction or utilization
of this work in whole or in part in any form by any electronic, mechanical or
other means, now known or hereafter invented, including xerography,
photocopying and recording, or in any information storage or retrieval system,
is forbidden without the permission of the publisher, Harlequin Enterprises
Limited, 225 Duncan Mill Road, Don Mills, Ontario, Canada M3B 3K9.

All the characters in this book have no existence outside the imagination of
the author and have no relation whatsoever to anyone bearing the same name
or names. They are not even distantly inspired by any individual known or
unknown to the author, and all incidents are pure invention.

® are Trademarks registered in the United States Patent and Trademark Office
and in other countries.

Printed in U.S.A.

CHAPTER ONE

'PLEASE be seated, ladies.'

The personnel manager flashed them a perfunctory smile. He waited until they were settled on the three chairs placed in front of his desk before sinking back into the far more comfortable chair behind it.

Ann glanced unobtrusively at the other two women, wondering what they felt about this unusual procedure. She had recognised them instantly as her rivals for the job, knew this would be the final interview, and hoped her qualifications had an edge on theirs. What she hadn't expected was for all three of them to be invited in to face the manager together.

Both women wore smooth, unruffled countenances. Ann had to concede that they were very smooth all over: their clothes smartly co-ordinated, make-up subtle, hair-styles chic and tidy. She wondered if she should have played herself up more, then emphatically discarded the thought. Until she knew what her new boss was like, it was better to be safe than sorry.

The personnel manager cleared his throat. A typical executive underling, Ann thought—pleased with himself for being a cog in a dynamic wheel, and determined to keep in step with the men above him. His cuff-links carried the company insignia and he emanated brisk efficiency from his short, neat haircut to his well-polished shoes.

He touched his gold-rimmed glasses before he spoke again, a mannerism Ann had noticed in her second interview. It had invariably preceded a question that carried more import than others. She did her best to relax and appear calmly confident.

'May I first congratulate all three of you?' he said, leading into a well-practised ego-stroke. 'It is no mean feat to have emerged from a meticulous screening of applicants as front runners for the position in question. However, you will appreciate that only one can be chosen, and that choice is not mine to make.'

He paused, obviously relishing the effect of his next statement. 'As you know, the position is that of confidential secretary, personal assistant, and girl Friday to one of our top executives. I may reveal to you now that the executive is Mr Fielding himself.'

Smiles broke out on the other women's faces, but Ann felt a momentary disquiet. Matthew Fielding had the reputation of being a high-roller in more ways than one. Certainly, he was one of the few astute businessmen whose methods of diversification had kept his company out of the stock-market crash of '87, and it would be exciting to work with a man of his stature and flair for making money. But he was also single and sexy, and made no secret of his appetite for beautiful women.

Ann hoped he kept his social life distinctly separate from his business one. She did not like womanisers. She would have much preferred a boss who was a committed family man. Although her experience with Bill Leyman's son-in-law clearly proved that some men left their marriage at home when they came to the office. There were all too few guarantees in life, Ann had found. Only those you made yourself.

But, career-wise, she could hardly look down her nose at the chance of being Matthew Fielding's personal assistant. That was the top rung of the ladder, and from there she could step just about anywhere—if she proved good enough.

'I trust you all understand that Mr Fielding is a very busy man,' the manager went on in an unctuous tone—a crawler, Ann thought, and wondered if she would be expected to crawl, too. 'He said to take you up to him when you'd all arrived, and naturally he will be the final arbiter. I'm sorry that two of you will inevitably be disappointed, but there it is...'

His hands lifted in a gesture that washed him of all responsibility, then he rose to his feet, all officious business.

'If you'll accompany me now...'

They trooped out to the elevators and were whizzed up to the top floor. Ann barely had time to take in the plush reception area—all peach and cream and a fabulous view over the city of Sydney from a huge picture window. The receptionist was a very attractive brunette who eyed all three of them in speculative appraisal as she confirmed that Mr Fielding was expecting them. Ann noticed the wedding ring on her left hand and wondered if it protected her from trouble. The personnel manager tapped on a door, opened it, and waved an arm for them to enter.

Ann hesitated. Surely he couldn't mean them all to go in at once? Surely Matthew Fielding would want to see them one at a time? The other two women stepped forward, and Ann earned a hurry-up frown for hanging back. Another general pep speech before the in-depth interview, she quickly reasoned, and followed the others. Their escort stepped in after them, closed the door quietly, and waited.

They all waited.

They were left standing in the middle of Matthew Fielding's office until he deigned to notice them. And, from the way he was sticking to the work on his desk, it looked as if paying some courteous attention to his visitors came a long way down on his list of priorities.

Busy and bloody rude, Ann thought, studying one of the foremost business brains in Australia with jaundiced eyes. Of course, she couldn't precisely see his brain through his thick black hair, but undoubtedly it was there, pulsing away as he continued to write whatever he was writing.

His eyebrows were rather thick and black, too. So were his eyelashes. His jaw looked as if it would wear a five o'clock shadow if he didn't shave twice a day. Definitely a hairy man, Ann decided, and she much preferred smooth-skinned ones.

Then he looked up, and Ann instantly knew how he got all the women he wanted. The eyes had it: dark brown and utterly riveting. They swept across the three of them and back to her.

'You in the grey suit...stay,' he commanded. Then, in just as sharp a tone of dismissal, 'Thank you for your time, ladies.'

And that was it!

His gaze dropped to the desk again and he went on writing.

Ann stood there like a stunned mullet while the personnel manager ushered the other two women out of the office and left with them. She couldn't believe—could hardly bring herself to believe—that at this top level of management any employee could be chosen like that. Just lined up as if it were a flesh parade, given barely a glance, and powee! That one!

The more she thought about it, the more insulting it was. Ann could feel herself burning with indignation—not only for herself, but for the other two women, too. Even though all three of them probably had equally viable qualifications, surely one could have shown she was likely to be a more compatible assistant than the others? But to be simply looked at and summarily dismissed...it showed no respect at all, not for abilities or anything.

Did he treat everyone like that...or just women?

The eyes flicked impatiently at her. 'Take a seat. I'll be with you in a minute.'

Ann sat, and studied him with considerable venom. She couldn't find any fault with his ears. But his nose wasn't perfect. It ski'd out a bit at the end. And his top lip was thin. Unfortunately that had the effect of making his fuller lower lip look provocatively sensual. His skin was deeply tanned. He would undoubtedly suffer from sun-cancers in the not too distant future. He was already thirty-eight.

Ann had picked that information up from a written profile on him when she had researched the company. He was also a fitness freak, encouraging all his employees to follow his example in keeping their bodies taut and terrific with healthy exercise. A slovenly body indicates a slovenly mind, et cetera. Which was a lot of rot, in Ann's opinion. She had met some very sharp minds that hadn't been encased in wonderful bodies, but it was not a point she would bother arguing, unless it became pertinent. She had no intention of joining a gym.

Nevertheless, she had to admit that Matthew Fielding looked exceptionally fit for a man of his age. Apart from his lower lip there was nothing soft about him. In fact, he was so emphatically a member of the opposite sex that he made Ann feel doubly conscious of being a woman.

And that led to the even more burning question ... why had he picked her out of the line-up?

The only part of her on show at all was her legs, and those only from the calf down. The grey suit was not designed to show off her femininity. The fine wool had been well-tailored, but the jacket fell loosely to her hips and the pleated skirt fell just as loosely from her waist. The white blouse she had chosen to wear with the suit had a high, narrow band around her long throat, quite Victorian in its modesty.

She had inherited her father's fine English skin, so she rarely bothered with make-up, except for a soft pink lipstick. Her rather vivid blue eyes were not so noticeable behind the owl-shaped glasses she had chosen to wear instead of the usual contact lenses. Her hair-style was eminently practical—a short bob cut to just below her ears and a fringe that brushed the top of her eyebrows. Her hair was fair, but not as startlingly so as when she was a child. The years had toned it into an average blonde colour.

Ann was satisfied that she had achieved a no-nonsense professional appearance. Not even the most decadent rake could look at her today and see any invitation for sex on the side. Unless he was the most perverse man on earth!

And she was not about to make the same mistake as she had in her last position—relaxing her guard so far that she had even told Bill Leyman about her mother. He had been very kind and fatherly—genuinely interested in her—and in her loneliness Ann had warmed to the old man.

It had been a real blow when he had announced his intention to retire. In her affection and loyalty to him, Ann had promised that she would stay on as personal assistant to his son-in-law, Roger Hopman, smoothing any upsets in the change-over. It had hurt her very deeply when she had discovered—so nastily—that Bill Leyman had not kept her confidence, and had told Roger Hopman about Ann's relationship to Chantelle.

From the very beginning Roger Hopman had antagonised her—blatantly staring at her breasts, her hips and her legs in obvious sexual speculation. It took away all Ann's pleasure in wearing nice clothes. And finally he had pounced, deriding her protests, justifying himself with those horribly sneering words—'like mother, like daughter'.

Ann had hit him—hit him in blind raging fury—and walked out.

She simmered with anger now, just thinking about it. But she felt reasonably sure that, whatever reason Matthew Fielding had for choosing her out of the line-up, it couldn't possibly have been for her physical attributes. And she would never be such a fool as to reveal her family background again! To anyone!

Matthew Fielding finally put his pen down and lifted his gaze. His eyes raked her from head to foot, and seemed to linger on the long, slim shapeliness of her legs before returning sharply to her face. Ann didn't move a muscle. She sat tight and prim. But every nerve in her body bristled with resentment.

'Your name?' he asked abruptly.

'Carmody, sir. Ann Carmody,' she replied, as coolly as she could.

His mouth quirked in appreciation. 'Nice voice, Carmody. I can live with that.'

She disdained to acknowledge the patronising compliment. No way in the wide world would he ever say that to a male employee. Why couldn't a woman ever be accepted on equal terms? She stared back frostily, vowing that she would teach this macho man to respect her abilities if it was the last thing she did.

'How old are you?' he asked.

'Twenty-eight, sir.'

'You don't look it.'

'I can produce my birth certificate if you require it, sir.' But she didn't want to. If he noticed that her Christian name was actually Angel, and not the shortened version she had given, he was just the type who would make some stupid joke about it.

'No. I'm sure it's all been checked,' he said wearily, and relaxed back into his top-executive chair. He regarded her broodingly from under lowered eyebrows. His teeth worried at his lower lip for several moments before he burst forth with more speech, obviously hating the words but driven to say them.

'I'll give it to you straight, Carmody. I want no female emotionalism in this office. We get on with the job. That's it. Do I make myself clear?'

Ann was mightily relieved to hear it, although she bridled at the suggestion that no woman could control her emotions. 'Certainly, sir,' she said with pointedly calm aplomb. 'You wish me to remain even-tempered at all times, no matter what the provocation.'

He grimaced. 'No, that's not what I mean. I am not unreasonable.' The eyes shot her a sharp, impatient look. 'But if you start this maudlin business of fancying yourself in love with me, you're out, Carmody. I will not be subjected to that again.'

Ann quickly swallowed an urge to laugh at his outrageous arrogance. Sex appeal he might have—on a very, very basic level—but he was far from irresistible when he was so full of himself. 'I see no difficulty there, sir,' she answered, poker-faced.

'Good!' he said, relief diluting some of his vexation. 'I have been so provoked by this idiotic situation that I was sorely tempted to hire a man this time. Except I wouldn't feel comfortable asking a man to...' He stopped and frowned.

'To make you coffee, sir?' Ann put in sweetly.

His hand waved in a disgruntled gesture. 'Things like that,' he admitted grudgingly, and the eyes bored into her with angry purpose. 'You're here to answer problems, not make them.'

Ann stared back at him fiercely, wanting to cut him down to size. He was her employer and she wanted nothing—absolutely nothing—of a more personal nature from him.

The unsavoury scandal that still clung to her mother's name had driven Ann out of one job. It gave her a certain perverse pleasure to pluck a line out of Chantelle's colourful life and use it to prune Matthew Fielding's colossal ego.

'I'm sure I won't trouble you, sir. Actually, I prefer younger men.'

His eyebrows rose in startled question. 'You do?'

Again Ann had to smother a laugh as his face underwent a conflict between affront and interested speculation.

'Well, they do have more...energy,' she said relentlessly. 'A man does tend to...um...flag a bit...as he gets older. No offence meant, of course,' she added soothingly. 'I'm sure you're an exception to every rule, sir. But I don't mind admitting my own—er—point of view, if it sets your mind at rest, sir.'

He nodded, but he didn't look particularly pleased with her revelation. 'I hope your...sexual athleticism with younger men...is not going to interfere with your work, Carmody. This is a very demanding job, as I'm sure you've been made aware.'

'The job comes first, sir,' she assured him solemnly, barely stopping the corners of her mouth from tugging into a smile. 'You will never have cause to complain about any indiscretions on my part,' she said with absolute sincerity. Then a wisp of unholy mischief made her add, 'Nor be concerned about my physical fitness. I exercise regularly and my mind is never less than sharp.'

'Fine!' he said with some asperity. 'I shall be fascinated to see what your sharp mind can make of this.' He leaned forward and tapped the sheet of paper he had been writing on. 'Here is a list of specific points I want considered in preparation for the company's annual convention, which is scheduled for a month's time. Arrange them into a memo that is easily read and understood. Check back with me when you've finished it.'

Ann rose from her chair in one gracefully fluid movement, walked to his desk, and was handed not one page, but a sheaf of papers.

His eyes glittered almost malicious challenge. 'Your office is through the door behind you, Carmody. All the equipment you need is in there—except your brain, which goes with you.'

Ann did not fear any challenge where work was concerned. It always fired her adrenalin to perform, and she relished the opportunity to make Matthew Fielding recognise and acknowledge that she was more than competent to deal with any task he tossed at her.

'When do you want it ready by, sir?' she asked matter-of-factly.

'Oh, let's see if you can manage a first draft by lunchtime,' he drawled. 'I would like it in the afternoon post.'

'Then, if you'll excuse me, sir, I'll get to work.'

Matt stared after her as she walked to the door which led to the adjoining office. Unbelievable! he kept thinking. The damned cheek of her! And still looking as prissy as if butter wouldn't melt in her mouth!

He had picked her because—at first glance—she had looked like a prim schoolteacher who had given up all idea of attracting a man, while the others were obviously barracuda career-women who'd be trying to run him instead of the other way around. And he didn't need the irritation of pulling them into line.

His pique gradually gave way to a wry admiration. He had to hand it to Carmody. She was as cool as a cucumber, which was what he needed in the office, even if she was a sex-bomb out of it. But she'd better deliver the goods after that snide little piece of one-upmanship!

He flicked through the three personnel files that had been placed on his desk that morning, found Carmody's, and leafed through it, picking up the salient points. She had done a three-year business course at Killara College, walked into a job in market research, and spent two years on that before moving into a large stockbroking company for one year. The last four years had seen her work her way up the corporate ladder of Leyman Commodities Pty. Ltd., and her last eighteen months there had been as personal assistant to Bill Leyman himself. She had resigned barely a month after the old man had handed the reins of his company over to his son-in-law.

Resigned before this job came on offer, Matt noted—only a fortnight or so—but it might be something that should be checked.

He turned to the references and read them with interest. Carmody's efficiency, integrity and initiative were highly praised, her resignation obviously regretted. Not the slightest word of criticism anywhere, which was only to be expected or she wouldn't have passed through the tight screening Matt had ordered.

Yet there was something about her—something elusive that niggled at Matt's mind. She might very well be Little Miss Perfect, and if she wasn't he would find out soon enough, but that wasn't the point. He liked to read his key employees like an open book, know them, catalogue them in his mind, and feel secure that they weren't going to surprise him by acting out of pattern.

And she had surprised him! Staggered him!

That cool air of discreet class that she effected had to be a false front if she indulged in the kind of sex romps she had suggested. Something was definitely wrong about her—something he needed to put his finger on.

He thought hard about it, disliking the idea of being at any disadvantage. It gradually dawned on him that she was the first woman in many years who had not so much as glanced at him with speculative interest. Amazing how financial success bred success with women, Matt thought cynically. He sometimes wondered if Janice would fall into his arms if he went back to her now. But he didn't want to know.

He had been played for a fool once, blinded by love into believing that Janice shared his dream. But when he had gambled everything on his first venture, and he had looked like going to the wall on it—where had the love and faith and support been then? Janice had made it brutally obvious that she'd been postponing their marriage until she was sure she was on to a winner, and when he had needed her most—well, as a lover he was great, but . . .

He would never be a fool over a woman again, Matt vowed bitterly. These days he had women falling over him, wanting to share his dream—or the fruits of it—but loving didn't enter into it, except the most basic kind of loving. And he could make do with that. After all, he had the intense satisfaction of extending his organisation with more and more successful ventures. A few more years and the company would have a turnover nearing a billion dollars. And, to him, that was achievement.

His mind slid automatically to the new project they were planning, and he reached for the research reports that had come in. They needed to move into the media—no doubt about that: newspapers, radio, television, communication, publicity . . .

Two hours later his concentration was interrupted by his new personal assistant, who pre-

sented him with a printed draft of the requested
memo.

'I think I have everything you want there, sir,'
she said in her pure, lilting voice.

Matt stared at her in surprise. Not because she
had done the work—however good or bad it was—
but because he hadn't noticed her eyes before. They
were as bright blue as cornflowers, and her skin
was astonishingly fine and flawless.

'You did say you wanted to check it before
lunchtime,' she reminded him with a definite touch
of pertness, pulling his attention down to the matter
in hand.

'Yes. Thank you,' he responded gruffly, and
frowned at the first page of the draft.

'I ran out a copy for myself, so if you'd like to
dictate any changes, I'll take note of them,' she said,
and sat herself down on the chair she had occupied
before.

Matt concentrated fiercely on the draft, page
after page of it. She had reorganised his points into
logical groupings, encapsulated his ideas in simple-
to-understand terms, and there wasn't even a typo
error, let alone a spelling mistake. He knew he
should be pleased, so he exerted his considerable
will-power to crush an irritating sense of having
been beaten.

'Fine job, Carmody. Keep this up and we'll get
on like a house on fire,' he said generously.

A faint smile flitted over her mouth, drawing his
attention to the generous lips. It was even more ir-

ritating to find they were perfectly shaped. Wasn't there anything imperfect about her?

'If you're satisfied, sir, shall I instruct the typing pool to do the envelopes, or...?'

'Yes,' he said briskly. 'And if you take the file-disc down to them, they can run off the required number of copies of the memo.'

'Anything else, sir?' she asked, rising to her feet.

'Then take your lunchbreak,' he instructed. 'We'll work on these reports this afternoon.'

As soon as she had gone Matt picked up the telephone and set about finding Bill Leyman. His curiosity, his need to pin that provocative woman down, was so compelling that he persisted through call after call until the old man was finally contacted at a holiday resort in North Queensland.

'Matt Fielding?' he squawked in surprise. 'What can I do for you? And don't forget you're talking to a retired man.'

'I'm after some information, Mr Leyman. About a Miss Carmody who worked for you.'

'Ann? Wonderful girl. Smart as paint. My company would probably have been better off if I'd installed her as the chairman of directors instead of my fool of a son-in-law, whose first claim to idiocy was to lose her very valuable know-how and services.'

'I hired her as my personal assistant this morning,' Matt put in.

'Lucky man. Start counting your blessings. That girl is worth her weight in gold.'

'I notice you wrote the reference, not your son-in-law,' Matt prompted.

'Ann came to me for it. Rightly so. She was my girl.' There was a slight hint of reserve in the reply, and even more when he added, 'Have you got a question, Matt?'

'I wondered why she left.'

There was a long pause. 'Nothing you need worry about, if you have the sense to play it straight with her. Ann likes to work. Keep that in mind and you'll keep her.'

'I don't think that answers my question. Could you be more direct?' Matt pressed.

A deep sigh whispered down the line. 'For her sake, I'll say it. I owe it to her. But this is in the strictest confidence. I don't want to hear it back, Matt. My company doesn't need that kind of rap. Ann left because of some very stupid sexual harassment. End of story.'

'Thank you. Be assured I'll respect your confidence. And I hope you enjoy your retirement.'

'No problem!' The old man laughed. 'Good luck, my boy, and don't burn yourself out making more money than you can enjoy. You only live once.'

'No problem,' Matt echoed good-humouredly, and hung up.

He relaxed back in his chair with a little chuckle of satisfaction. Everything was fine—in place. The whole irony of this morning's exchange with Carmody bore down on him, and he laughed outright.

He had been warning her off, and she had been doing exactly the same thing to him!

He wondered if her sexual athleticism with younger men was a cock and bull story. Not that it mattered. And whatever the truth of *her* experience, *he* certainly wasn't flagging. Mitzi could attest to that. Thirty-eight wasn't old. He was in the prime of life. And he was enjoying the success he had made of it. Retirement was a long way away. There were more mountains to climb, more . . .

He wondered what Carmody looked like underneath that shapeless grey suit.

CHAPTER TWO

SHE had fixed him, Ann thought with gleeful triumph. She had hoist him with his own petard and he had squirmed beautifully. And serve him right!

She couldn't repress a giggle at the memory of his expression when she had said she preferred younger men. The man sitting next to her in the train threw her a startled glance, then looked around the compartment to see if he could pick up what was so funny. Ann bit her lip and tried to sober up. Not that she had been drinking. She would never touch a drop of alcohol. She was simply intoxicated with success.

Firstly, she had got the job. Secondly, she had put Matthew Fielding in his place—he could be her boss, but not anything else. Thirdly, she had forced him to re-evaluate and respect her worth when she had shown him what she could do with his memo. Then after lunch it had been a whole new ball game. And a fascinating one, too.

The man was brilliant. The way he had dissected those reports this afternoon was almost awesome. He cut straight to the heart of every problem, re-defined its parameters, and struck out in unexpected but astute directions in order to provide answers.

No doubt about it now—Matthew Fielding was exciting to work with. She had got carried away a bit, offering a few suggestions of her own. That had startled him, too, but to his credit he had shown no male chauvinism at all in considering her ideas fairly and appreciatively. And accepting them.

'You can think, Carmody,' he had said, with the kind of respect Ann valued. She had almost smiled at him, only catching back the natural response at the last moment. No way was she going to give him any cause to think that she fancied him.

Which, of course, she didn't!

Those eyes of his were not going to get to her.

The train pulled in at Wollstonecraft Station. Ann jumped up and hurriedly pushed her way past the standing passengers. She just made it out to the platform before the exit doors shut. And that came from letting her mind become so preoccupied with thoughts of Matthew Fielding!

But she had made it. Today she had really made it! Personal assistant to Matthew Fielding!

She didn't even feel the chilly August wind. A wave of warm exultation carried her up the pathway to her apartment block and right into her flat. Her gaze swept lovingly around the photographs of her mother, and a sudden well of emotion brought tears to her eyes.

'I won today, Mum,' she said, instinctively fighting back any weakness. She walked across the

living-room and picked up her favourite photograph—one she had taken herself—of Chantelle
smiling her love without a trace of professionalism.
No star of stage and television—just her mother.
'I struck a blow for you as well as me,' she added
softly.

Her sadness was difficult to contain as she stared
down at the beautiful face—Chantelle, who had
wanted to be loved by everyone. Younger men had
helped convince her she would never really grow
old. She was beautiful, desirable, lovable. And she
had laughingly thrown away that line about men
flagging as they grew older—flagging as she never
would.

As much as she had hated her mother's world,
Ann had loved her mother. Chantelle had always
wanted the best for everyone, wanted to believe the
best of everyone. She had lived her fantasy world,
clung to it beyond reason and reality, but she had
always had loving time for her daughter, her very
own Angel.

Ann was not ashamed of her mother. She had
been a truly good person, doing no harm to anyone
except to herself. What Ann hated was the way
people remembered her, because of her death. Sex
and drugs and the taint of debauchery. And it had
only been another stupid mistake. A stupid, trusting
mistake. Making life lovely and beautiful, as it
should be. But no one understood that. No one
except Ann.

She heaved a deep sigh and replaced the photograph. Her hand automatically reached out and switched on the hi-fi equipment. Music was her solace and her pleasure, one of the joys she had shared with her mother. It always helped diminish the private loneliness in her life.

And today she had cause to celebrate, cause to be happy and satisfied, not sad. Ann selected the compact disc of the latest musical she had bought, slotted it into the player, and waltzed off to her bedroom as the overture moved into full swing.

The grey suit was hung carefully in the wardrobe. The white blouse went into the laundry basket in the bathroom. Ann pushed her arms into the brilliant silk housecoat she favoured at the moment—the print of poppies in bloom was very cheerful—then headed for the kitchen to prepare her evening meal.

The musical moved into the opening song and Ann joyously lifted her own voice to join in. She knew all the words by heart—every word in the whole score—and loved singing along. It was her greatest pleasure.

Sometimes she envied the singers and wondered if she had made the wrong choice—wondered if she should have gone on and done what her mother had urged her to do. Perhaps she had been wrong to turn her back on the world her parents had occupied. But that world had destroyed first her father and then her mother. It was an insecure, driven kind of life, filled with glittering highs and desperate lows—nothing stable or reliable about it.

At least she could control the career she had chosen. It depended on no one but herself. And she was good at it. She would soon show Matthew Fielding just how good she was—show him that a woman was good for something besides jumping into bed with him, or lusting for him to jump into bed with her.

Ann stopped singing. Her mouth set in belligerent determination. She was never going to let a need for sex degrade her standards. Messy business, anyway. She really had no need for it at all. It was much less wear and tear on the nerves to keep the whole thing at bay.

It was clear now that the grey suit had served her well this morning. She couldn't have looked less like a woman who was stalking a man. All she had to do was maintain that image, and Matthew Fielding would get the message that, as a man, he left her completely cold.

Tomorrow she would spend her lunchbreak hunting out two more unflattering grey suits—the more shapeless and dull, the better. They would form her office uniform, along with a number of primly styled blouses. What she wore underneath was an entirely different matter, and it gave Ann a delicious sense of mischief to think of completely stodgy clothes covering up the exquisitely feminine lingerie that was one of her private passions.

She had probably inherited her taste for exotic clothes from her mother. Unfortunately, in her chosen walk of life Ann had few occasions to wear them. Sometimes she regretted that she had not been born in another century. In the normal course of things, modern clothes allowed one very little in the way of rich and stunning extravagance. Show business was the exception, of course, but that was not for her. Definitely not.

Nevertheless, it would amuse her to dress up for Matthew Fielding. In a totally negative way. It was one blow she could strike for her own convictions! He would be forced to recognise her value as a person, not as a *woman*.

As it turned out, however, he struck the first blow the next morning.

Against Ann's cherished sense of self-worth!

He didn't even give her the courtesy of a greeting.

'Ah! I've been waiting for you,' he said in an impatient tone the moment she arrived. 'I need coffee. The makings are in your office. I take it black. No sugar. Hurry it up, will you?'

'Yes, sir. Good morning, sir,' Ann replied with sweet acid.

Her tone and subtle rebuff sailed right over his head. He kept on working.

She made the coffee—grudgingly—and carried it to his desk. 'I hope that's strong enough for you, sir,' she said, having deliberately made it weak. After all, he hadn't given her instructions to the contrary. He had treated her like a servant who should know all her master's whims and overlook his rudeness. Obviously he needed to be taught a lesson!

He glanced up with a frown of irritation. 'Carmody, I am not a schoolmaster. Cut the *sir* business.'

'I'm sorry, sir.'

'For heaven's sake, Carmody!' he snarled.

Ann's face gave blandness a new meaning. 'It's simply an automatic response to an authority-figure, Mr Fielding. You see, you remind me of my father——'

'Enough!' he snapped, then dragged in a deep breath. 'Just go and get on with the mail I left on your desk.'

'Yes, Mr Fielding,' Ann said emphatically, and moved off very smartly, aware that she had tried his patience to the limit. But he had asked for it, treating her like a lackey who didn't even deserve the minimum of good manners.

She started on the mail.

Matthew Fielding appeared in her doorway ten minutes later, cup and saucer in hand. 'This is dish-water, Carmody,' he growled.

Ann looked up in puzzlement. 'Dish-water, sir?'

He sighed. Heavily. 'Make my coffee double this strength in future.'

'Oh! Sorry, sir. I'll get it right next time,' she promised solemnly.

'See that you do,' he grated, then banged the cup and saucer down on her desk and stalked off.

A worm of guilt wriggled into Ann's conscience. For all she knew, he might have been at his desk for hours before she had arrived—preoccupied with some thorny problem or other. Perhaps she had been over-critical about his lack of greeting and the request for coffee.

After all, most secretaries were expected to supply coffee on demand from their bosses. And since the makings were in her office, she could have a cup herself whenever she liked. She wasn't being fair-minded about it. And Ann prided herself on her fair-mindedness. In future, she would certainly make his coffee precisely as he liked it.

But she felt totally unrepentant about the 'sir' business. When he stopped acting like a schoolmaster, she might relent. But, until then, he could hardly fire her for respectful deference to his authority. Nevertheless, she wouldn't push her luck to any foolish extreme.

She really should try to curtail her urge to hit back at Matthew Fielding every time he aroused her ire. It wasn't his fault that she was still smarting over her experience with Roger Hopman, and this job was certainly worth suffering a little bit of heartburn now and then.

Having made that resolution, Ann was careful to mix plenty of 'Mr Fielding's in with only a moderate number of 'sir's when they had to converse about the business in hand. At eleven o'clock he announced that he had a dental appointment and told her to deal with any calls for him until he returned.

Ann was quite happy to do so—the perfect secretary and personal assistant in action—until the Mitzi call!

'I want Matt,' the sexy voice breathed down the line. 'Tell him it's Mitzi.'

'I'm afraid Mr Fielding is out at the moment, and I'm not sure when he will return,' Ann explained, mentally attaching a voluptuous body to the voice, and gritting her teeth as she added, 'Would you like to leave a message?'

After some irritating musing and a positively salacious laugh, Mitzi came up with a message that had Ann burning with fury at being used as a go-between in Matthew Fielding's sex-life. Her pen almost stabbed through the notepad as she wrote it down.

Lover-boy returned just before noon. Ann had tried to simmer down, but to little avail. Business was business. He had said it himself—no female emotionalism in this office. We get on with the job. That's it. And here he was—on the first day!— dragging her into his personal intimacies. That kind of assistant he could look for elsewhere!

Determined to let him know it one way or another, Ann brought him the list of calls, each notated on a separate page.

'Read them out to me,' he ordered brusquely. 'And add any comments you consider pertinent.'

Ann dealt with the business calls first. Having been given an invitation to pass comment, she did so, relishing the opportunity he had unwittingly given her.

'The last call was from Mitzi. She said to thank you for the flowers, and to tell you she had hay fever——'

He frowned. 'Hay fever?'

'Yes, sir.' Ann deliberately kept her voice flat and matter-of-fact. 'A fever for another roll in the hay with you, sir. Any time.'

His grin was obscenely smug.

If he had looked bored or irritated, Ann might have held her tongue. She couldn't exactly blame him for Mitzi's initiative. But, faced with his smug pleasure in his womanising, Ann suffered a wild rush of blood to the head.

So he thought he was God's gift to women, did he? That every one of them was ready to fall flat on her back for him at any time of the day or night? Just because he was wealthy and good-looking and had a certain animal magnetism. And he had even had the gall to warn her off!

Her sense of discretion was crushed by an overwhelming need to give him feet of clay. 'Apparently you were very satisfactory, sir,' she commented, completely dead-pan.

It wiped out the grin.

'I do not need your appraisal on my private life, Carmody,' he advised her coldly.

'You did ask for comment, sir. I was trying to oblige.'

He glowered at her. 'Trying, Carmody? You have some doubts about this message?'

Ann frowned in consideration. 'Voices can be deceptive, sir. But Mitzi did sound satisfied.' She brightened. 'Perhaps it would be better if you directed such personal calls to your home. Then you would be sure to get them yourself and be able to use your own judgement.'

He looked as if steam would emerge from his ears any moment. His gaze ran a blistering trail down her shapeless grey suit and up again. 'No doubt you are well-versed in the sound of satisfaction,' he said acidly.

'I can't honestly lay claim to that, sir,' Ann said with absolute candour. 'I'm more accustomed to the sound of men's satisfaction than women's. I'm sure your experience would be a better basis for judgement, sir.'

'That will do, Carmody,' he said with ominous quiet. 'You may go to lunch now.'

'Thank you, sir.'

Ann smiled to herself as she sped into town to the department stores which carried the largest range of ready-to-wear suits. The thought of Matthew Fielding listening critically for the sound of satisfaction next time he was bedding one of his women tickled her sense of humour. And soothed her bruised ego. She doubted that he would care to have her answering calls from his lady-loves again.

However, as the days passed, Ann found there was one rather vexatious consequence from her vanity-pricking manoeuvres.

She enjoyed her new job, enjoyed the confidence that Matthew Fielding began to place in her abilities, enjoyed the challenge of keeping up with his ideas and business initiatives. And she had no quarrel with his manner towards her. He kept his hands to himself and limited all conversation between them to the work in hand. But from time to time she caught him looking at her—no, staring at her—in a most disconcerting and disturbing fashion.

The moment she caught him at it, he would say something to suggest that his gaze had been abstracted while his mind was revolving a problem, but it didn't feel like that. It felt as if he had been mentally stripping her of her clothes.

She began to wish she hadn't said that nonsense about preferring younger men, or made the suggestive remark that she knew the sound of men's satisfaction. Although the latter was true enough, in the context of work. Nevertheless, the idea of him speculating about her . . . like that . . . made her skin crawl.

To make any objection to it was impossible. She could just imagine his reaction. He would instantly accuse her of weaving fantasies about him, wanting him to notice her. But she knew her feeling was right the day the dress-shirt affair occurred.

'I need a new dress-shirt for tonight,' he stated at the end of a hard morning's work. 'Take extra time with your lunch-break and pick one up for me, Carmody. Size sixteen.'

'You want me to buy you a dress-shirt?' Ann said flatly, wanting to believe he wasn't serious.

He frowned at her. 'Size sixteen,' he repeated, as if she might have missed it the first time.

'Sixteen,' she echoed through fast clenching teeth. 'And where do you shop, sir?'

He shot her an impatient look. 'I don't shop, Carmody. That's your job.'

Ann counted to five. A lot of bosses asked their secretaries to pick up their dry-cleaning, or buy presents, or do some errand or other that was totally unrelated to their jobs. That was a fact of life. It didn't matter that every secretary Ann had ever spoken to hated doing such chores. It was still demanded of them. But shopping for Matthew Fielding's clothes was one step too far!

'I don't recall that being in the job specification, sir,' she said, the fire in her head reduced to ice off her tongue.

One eyebrow rose in mocking challenge to her tone. 'Personal assistant, Carmody. Do I have to underline the personal?'

Ann seethed—there were a lot of shades of *personal* that were way out of line as far as she was concerned—but she somehow managed to keep her temper in check. 'Dress-shirt. Size sixteen,' she recited, and swept out of the office before she threw her handbag at him.

Sexist pig! she raged. This was why he had hired a woman instead of a man. But she would give him his come-uppance with a vengeance. If Matthew Fielding thought she would fill in as a pseudo-wife, he had another think coming.

Ann picked out the most ostentatious dress-shirt she could find. Frills galore. And, to her intense satisfaction, he didn't even look inside the packet when she handed it to him, taking it for granted that she had got him what he wanted. As she always did in the office.

The next morning he was in a foul mood when she arrived for work: slumped in his chair, feet on the desk, his hands angrily snapping pencils and hurling the bits into a metal waste-paper bin. Clang—rattle—thunk! Clang—rattle—thunk!

'And how are we this morning?' he bit out sarcastically, eyes glowering.

'Fine, thank you, sir,' Ann trilled back at him.

'Not troubled with your Jekyll and Hyde characters?'

'Pardon, sir?'

The feet crashed down from the desk and he stalked around it to confront her, all bristling macho manhood. 'Look at me, Carmody,' he thundered. 'Take a good, long look.'

Ann calmly obliged by running her eyes up and down his impressive six-foot frame. 'Yes, sir?' she prompted, while he still continued to glower at her.

'I wear plain white shirts, Carmody. I wear quiet, tasteful ties. I wear conservative suits.' His voice rose several decibels. 'I am not the kind of man who enjoys looking like a ruffled peacock! And I had no other option last night but to wear that ridiculous dress-shirt you bought me.'

'Ridiculous?' Ann echoed with limpid innocence. 'I thought it was very nice.'

'Nice!' he squawked. 'Have you no taste at all?' His eyes sliced down her clothes with gathering venom. 'That was, perhaps, a stupid question,' he drawled nastily. 'Don't you have anything else in your wardrobe besides that grey sack suit? You've worn it every damned day!'

Ann's private satisfaction in her tactical manoeuvre died on the spot. 'It may have escaped your notice, sir,' she said frigidly, 'but I have three different grey suits—similar in style—which have proved to be eminently practical for my purpose. If you have some objection, sir, apart from your distaste for my choice——'

'You're a woman!' he shouted at her. 'What the hell do you think you're proving by dressing like a man?'

'I know what I am, Mr Fielding. And I don't have to prove I'm a woman to you or anyone else. That is certainly not part of my job specification. Indeed, sir, you went out of your way to tell me you wanted no female nonsense in this office. Did I get you wrong, sir? Or didn't you say precisely what you meant?'

She could hear his teeth grating as he replied with slow biting emphasis. 'Carmody, I promise you, I shall not presume you've set your sights on me if you wear a dress.'

Stubbornness, egged on by fierce resentment, formed Ann's glacial retort. 'I prefer to wear my suits, sir.'

'Fine!' His eyes snapped at her as well as his voice. 'That's fine by me! But in future, do not buy me ruffled dress-shirts. Or ruffled anything!'

He turned abruptly and stalked back behind his desk, every stride emanating pent-up frustration. His hands were clenched, and Ann prickled with the thought that he had wanted to grab her and shake her. He was, without a doubt, a very physical man, and there was a distinct air of violence about him as he dropped into his chair and glared balefully at her.

'Just tell me one thing, Carmody. It could be the last thing you tell me.'

He paused to let that sink in. Pure malevolence, Ann thought, bristling against the dominance he projected over her fate. There were other jobs— probably not with the same status and interest as this one, but she was not so tied to his star that she couldn't find satisfaction elsewhere.

'If you prefer those...suits...' he continued acidly '...which would have to be the last word in conservatism, how did you come to choose that frilly abomination for me?'

She could resign here and now, but the urge to beat this arrogant male chauvinist was totally compelling. She did not allow one muscle of her face to move. She returned his glare with a steady, serene gaze and spoke with calm, cool reason.

'I have no taste, sir. You said so yourself. Might I suggest, sir, that you delegate someone else to do your shopping? It would save us both any further disharmony in our working relationship.'

He smiled. Grimly. As if he were stretching the corners of his mouth out to show her that absolute control was his, and his alone. 'I'm sure you won't repeat the mistake, Carmody,' he said in a soft voice that spelled danger with every syllable spoken. 'I have great faith in your powers to grasp any concept.'

Her chin lifted. No matter what the consequences, she had to fight him. She was not going to let him get away with this. But she was not going to throw away the job, either. She felt as if she were negotiating a very narrow bridge which differentiated victory from defeat. She chose her words with great care.

'I'm afraid, sir, that your faith in my taste is misplaced in this particular instance. My conventional choice you consider drab and boring. Apart from that I have an obsessional weakness for rather exotic clothes outside of work. This I unfortunately revealed in choosing your . . . frilly abomination. I'm sorry, sir, but I really do think that proves my judgement is unreliable.'

Her argument was impeccably logical. Matthew Fielding looked as if he were suffering from lockjaw. 'Damn it, Carmody! We're wasting time!' he burst out in frustration. Then, in the twinkling of an eye, his expression changed. His eyebrows rose in speculative interest. 'What kind of exotic clothes, Carmody?' he asked, his voice dripping with fascinated curiosity.

Trust him to pick that little item out of her speech! His eyes seemed to light with all manner of possibilities as they travelled over her body, seeking vantage points to hang his imagination on.

Damn him! Damn him! Damn him! Ann railed in fuming silence. It was her own fault for raising the spectre, but he needn't be so...so perverse about it! She took a deep breath to calm her jumping pulse.

'If you'll excuse me, sir, you did say we were wasting time. There's that report you requested yesterday waiting on my desk, and——'

'Yes, yes,' he said impatiently, his eyes still roving in intrigued speculation. 'Let me see it when you've finished.'

Ann should have felt relief that the battle was over and, if she hadn't won it, she had certainly given him pause for thought. Unfortunately, his thoughts were not exactly running along the lines she wanted. Tactical retreat was in order. At least she had survived to fight again.

It took every smidgen of Ann's control to turn her back on him and walk to her adjoining office with poise and dignity, but she did it. Then she sat at her desk and silently called Matthew Fielding every venomous name she could think of.

He had been positively blatant about doing it just now, but he had been doing it all along—reducing her to a body. It was how he thought of women. Just sexual objects and serving-girls. But let him try any more of it on her! Just let him try! She would make him pay through the nose, and every other vulnerable part of his anatomy, too!

CHAPTER THREE

ANN slowly relaxed over the next two weeks. It seemed that Matthew Fielding's blow-up over the clothes issue was a closed episode. He didn't ask her to do any more shopping for him, and he didn't look at her in anything but a straight and acceptable fashion. There were no more calls from his lady-loves, or if there were he answered them himself.

They actually got on very well together. On a purely business level, they forged a quick and mutually satisfying understanding. Planning for the forthcoming convention took up most of their time. Two hundred employees from all branches of the company were to be given a general overlook of all the business initiatives in progress, and encouraged to find applications for those initiatives in their own areas of responsibility.

Ann liked the way Matthew Fielding involved everyone in his moves towards bigger and better business. It engendered the sense of sharing in the success of the company. By way of relenting her initial antagonism she would have called him 'Mr Fielding' all the time, except occasionally she felt impelled to keep a very definite distance between them.

Like when he smiled at her.

Or when his eyes danced in triumph at finding a way to do what he wanted.

She had to admit he was attractive. Probably the most attractive man she had ever met. But in a very limited way, of course. Outside of business, his character was totally unattractive to her. Ann kept that firmly in mind.

She loved her office. It was a lot smaller than Matthew Fielding's, but furnished in the same style: a peachy-cream carpet, Scandinavian-type furniture in blonde wood, comfortable chairs. Even the filing cabinets and her personal computer with its accompanying laser printer were a toning cream colour. Her view from the window was not quite as good as the harbour view from his office, but she was not about to complain. She felt privileged to have it.

As she had done in every place where she had worked, Ann quickly formed a friendly acquaintance with the various women she met on the staff. She was extremely cautious about close friendships—having Chantelle as her mother had drawn people to Ann in the past, not always with happy results—but she was far from antisocial, and enjoyed the company of other women. More so than the company of men. Which was probably a hangover from having been educated at an all-girls' school.

She found the receptionist, Sarah Dennis, particularly nice, although they had few interests in common. Sarah was married, with two school-age children, and she was obsessed with interior decoration. She and her husband were renovating an old house they had bought, and she rarely talked about anything else.

Ann asked her once about the women who had previously held her position. 'I never gossip about Mr Fielding's business,' Sarah stated unequivocally. 'He doesn't like it, and I like my job.'

She paused, eyed Ann warningly, and added, 'All I'll say is this—I never saw him give them any encouragement, and I've heard him say that a man who muddies his own nest is a fool. If you want my advice, don't fall in love with him. You're only asking for trouble.'

Ann laughed, to set Sarah's mind at ease. 'I'm not after trouble,' she assured her, and smoothly moved the conversation back to home renovation.

However, Matthew Fielding's maxim—'a man who muddies his own nest is a fool'—gave Ann a pleasant reassurance. It was probably the reason why he had snapped himself out of looking at her with that discomfiting speculation. Besides which, she was sure he no longer saw her as a *woman* so much as a mind that was tuned to his.

And he was great to work with. He rarely wasted a moment, and his energy level was amazing. Meetings were conducted with incredible efficiency. He went through paperwork like a threshing machine. It was a heady experience for

Ann to keep up with him, and an even headier one if she anticipated his needs.

She began to understand the unique qualities that had taken him from being a financial journalist in his early twenties to a millionaire businessman by his early thirties, buying into shaky enterprises and turning them into almost overnight successes. His drive and confidence would inspire anybody, and his ability to deliver profits had been proven over and over again.

She could not help but admire him. In a purely objective sense. She was ultra-careful never to show him admiration in case he interpreted it wrongly, or took advantage of it, as he almost certainly would in his male-chauvinist way.

Work became more hectic and tightly concentrated as the scheduled convention drew nearer. Ann was secretly looking forward to it as her first big challenge. Matthew Fielding had made her responsible for seeing that what he wanted done was done. Quite a tall order, when he was such a perfectionist over even the smallest detail. But Ann was sure she could do it. And a week at the Mirage Hotel on the Gold Coast would be a fine experience, even though she would be working most of the time.

The Mirage was reputedly one of the best hotels in Australia, five-star international standard, and the brochure on it heightened her anticipation. The architecture looked fantastic, and the landscaped grounds were a tropical dream. Warm sunshine would also be a pleasant change from Sydney's bleak winter weather.

Only nine more days, Ann thought happily, but she quickly wiped the musing smile off her face when Matthew Fielding entered her office. She didn't want to invite an accusation of day-dreaming, and his expression was harassed.

'I need you to work with me this weekend, Carmody. There's too much to get done on my own, and time's running out,' was his blunt announcement.

It didn't worry Ann. She had no special plans for the weekend. 'That's all right, Mr Fielding,' she answered equably. 'What time will you want me in the morning?'

'Not here. You'll have to come with me to Fernlea. That's my country home, a couple of hours north from Sydney. We'll leave here at four-thirty. We can stop at your place on the way for you to pack a bag. Wollstonecraft, isn't it?'

'Mmm...' Ann hummed distractedly. She had read about Fernlea. Colonial-type mansion... horses...but the question jagging through her mind centred fair and square on the man in front of her. She had everything comfortably settled in the office environment, but she instinctively shied away from sharing Matthew Fielding's home with him.

'This is not an invitation to a dirty weekend, Carmody,' he said sardonically, snapping her attention back to him. 'It's work. And you won't have to worry about a chaperon. My mother lives there.'

'Yes, sir,' Ann acknowledged, while her mind sought furiously for a way to escape the personal intimacy of a family weekend. 'What about your mother? You can't just land me on her. Is there somewhere nearby that I can stay?'

His eyes withered her argument. 'It's *my* home, Carmody. What I say goes. I've got enough hassles without you adding to them by not being at hand when I want you.'

He walked back into his office before Ann could think of any other protests. She realised, after a few minutes' stewing over the situation, that none of them would have prevailed, anyway. She could only hope that the house was large enough for her to keep out of Matthew Fielding's way when they were not working. She found the idea of a less than businesslike encounter with him profoundly disturbing.

Four-thirty came, and Matthew Fielding collected her on the dot. They took the elevator down to the basement car park in silence. He ushered her to his black Porsche and helped her into the passenger seat with impersonal courtesy. Ann was intensely relieved when he released his light grasp on her arm. She didn't want him touching her.

'Thank you,' she muttered, more for the release than the attention.

'All women need looking after,' he said in a perfunctory way.

Ann burned. His assumed superiority was hard to swallow in silence. She only just managed it, while berating her own stupidity for feeling so physically conscious of him. They had worked closely together for weeks. There was nothing different about this. Just because he took her arm...it was the kind of thing Matthew Fielding did automatically with any woman. Male chauvinists clung to chivalry and courtesy as bulwarks against the rise of equality.

He stowed his attaché case behind the driver's seat, settled himself behind the wheel, and closed his door. Regardless of all the reasoning that marched through Ann's mind, there seemed to be an intimacy in sitting beside him in his plush sports car that she had never felt in the larger confines of either of their offices. She was intensely aware of him and his every movement as he drove out into the traffic stream heading for the bridge.

'Incidentally, my mother's name is not Fielding. It's Mallory. Second marriage. And widowed twice,' he stated matter-of-factly, then sliced her a dry look. 'You can have tonight off. She wants to talk to me. Tomorrow will be high pressure. I want to get through as much as we can before my sister descends on us with her brood.'

No comment seemed required, so Ann made none. But her mind squirmed at the thought of being forced to mix with his family. She really did not want to see or know Matthew Fielding outside their work situation. She had him neatly categorised now—everything under control—and she did not want the current smoothness of their working relationship to be disturbed by a change in its limits. She wanted the emphasis kept on the *assistant* part, not the *personal* one. However, it seemed this weekend was a necessary evil.

'You'll need to pack a dinner-dress,' he said. 'There's to be a birthday dinner for my sister to-morrow night. Semi-formal.'

'I'd rather not——'

'This is work, Carmody,' he said with acid emphasis.

Ann frowned at him, but his gaze remained fixed on the traffic ahead. Did he have to involve her in a family dinner-party where she would surely be the odd person out? She supposed it would be rude to decline since she was a guest in the house.

'A little bit of exotica will not be out of place,' he added. 'A grey suit certainly would be. Apart from which, I'd like to see an example of how bad your taste really is.'

Ann's eyes sharpened on him. He did not glance at her. His gaze remained steady on the road. But his mouth was twitching in irrepressible amusement.

The sneaky low-down rat! He was getting back at her for the shirt. He wasn't going to be beaten by a woman. That was what this weekend was all about! His monumental male ego demanded he get the better of her.

Ann's bitter heartburn gradually simmered down enough to allow a more balanced viewpoint. The job certainly came first with him. This had to be a side issue. But Matthew Fielding liked to be a winner. At everything!

And the hell of it was, she now had to justify her argument to him. Hoist with her own petard, she thought with a rapidly sinking heart. If she didn't wear something exotic, she didn't have a hope of sticking to her guns in the shopping battle, which she now realised was merely in abeyance, waiting to be rejoined at a more tactical time.

She had admired his mind and his tenacity. He never gave up on anything unless he was firmly convinced there was no way around a problem. But she was not about to give up, either.

'It is country, not city, sir. I do think it would be safer if I wore my suit,' she warned.

'Then my mother and sister would scold me for not having instructed you properly,' he argued smugly. 'No, Carmody. I won't be put in the dog-house with my family. It's party-time, and grey suits are out.'

She heaved a deep sigh. 'You may regret this instruction, Mr Fielding. But so be it, if you say so.'

'I say so,' he iterated firmly.

What did she care what his mother and sister thought of her? She didn't know them. They meant nothing to her. And he had just taken responsibility for her choice, after fair warning had been given. It was all his fault and he couldn't criticise her, no matter what she wore.

Battle was rejoined.

Ann's mind shot to the cheongsam she had bought in Hong Kong on her last holiday. If he wanted to see exotica, she would give it to him in bucketfuls. And it would make him think twice about challenging her taste in clothes again.

Her mouth began to twitch in irrepressible amusement.

'Direct me,' he barked at her as they approached Wollstonecraft, and Ann quickly turned her attention to navigating his car on to the most time-efficient route to her apartment block.

They were fortunate enough to get a parking spot right outside the front entrance. 'I won't be long,' Ann tossed at him as she removed the seat-belt and opened her door.

'No need to rush,' he said, and to her consternation he opened his own door and alighted from the car.

Ann stared at him over the low-slung bonnet, a sudden and unnerving suspicion pumping through her heart. 'Where are you going?' she blurted out.

'I'm coming with you to carry your bag,' he said equably.

A chill ran through Ann's bones. She couldn't let him into her apartment. He would see the photographs of her mother, and he would probe. He would want to know the connection. And it was none of his business!

'That's not necessary. I'll carry my own bag,' she argued.

She saw the battle-light spark into his eyes, and knew he was piqued by her refusal to accept his offer. He leant his arms on the bonnet and his eyes simmered at her over it.

'Carmody, you may live by your lights. I shall live by mine. I open doors for ladies. I carry ladies' bags. I realise you're stuffed full of the women's liberation credo. To a certain degree, I will tolerate it—as long as it doesn't interfere with my way of doing things.'

She didn't move. She had to stop him somehow. Every intuitive nerve she possessed screamed that to let Matthew Fielding into her private life was to shatter the control she kept on their relationship. She saw his belligerence shift to speculative curiosity, and knew she had to say something.

'Very well, sir. If you must insist, you may carry my bag. But please don't expect me to invite you into my apartment. That is my *private* domain,' she said with fierce emphasis.

His mouth quirked sardonically, but his eyes hardened. 'Hiding something, Carmody? A stack of younger men under the bed, perhaps?'

She flinched at the nasty barb, but the issue was too critical for her to care what he thought. Misdirected speculation was infinitely better than letting him discover the truth. Normally, if she invited anyone to her home, she put the photographs away beforehand. She hated the type of curiosity they aroused. And, no matter what Matthew Fielding

said now, she was not going to open that door to
him.

'You go too far, sir,' she said quietly.

Whether it was her tone of voice or whether her
acute sense of vulnerability showed in her eyes, Ann
did not know. She saw him check himself, frown
in vexation, then, to her considerable amazement
and relief, he backed down. And did it with
considerable grace.

'So I do,' he agreed with a rueful grimace. 'In
fact, I apologise. That was uncalled for. You have
every right to the privacy of your home. Go ahead,
Carmody. I'll wait for you here.'

Ann's heart was beating painfully fast as she
hurried away. Her home . . . his home . . . she didn't
like any of it. If this weekend was going to be a
series of personal clashes with Matthew Fielding,
Ann was not at all sure she could keep her cool.
She was used to working under pressure—even enjoyed it—but usually she could leave work behind
and relax how she liked. That was clearly going to
be impossible, staying in Matthew Fielding's home.

She felt pressured even while she packed, her
mind skating through possible traps. If her room
at Fernlea did not have an en suite bathroom, which
was more than likely, she might get caught in a
hallway. She had to look exotic outside of work.
The dragon housecoat went into her suitcase, along
with the cheongsam. Day-wear was definitely a grey
suit, so she chose a couple of clean blouses to wear
with it. And walking shoes, in case she could escape

the household for a while. When she finally zipped her case shut, Ann hoped she had thought of everything.

When she emerged from the building she found Matthew Fielding pacing the pavement, his expression clearly one of annoyance with himself. The moment he caught sight of her, his face tightened up into a reserved mask. He strode forward to take Ann's suitcase from her. Without saying a word, he saw her seated in the car, stowed the bag in the boot, and resumed his place behind the wheel.

The moment they were on their way he started discussing business with her, and it was just as if they were back in the office together without any conflict of personalities or beliefs.

Ann gradually relaxed. Maybe the weekend wouldn't be so bad, after all. She should look on the bright side of things. It would be a change from the city, anyway. And she could hardly look down her nose at staying in a country mansion with good food and pleasant surroundings. As long as Matthew Fielding stayed in his 'boss mode' with her, there was really very little to worry about.

CHAPTER FOUR

DARKNESS had fallen before they reached Fernlea, so Ann saw little more than the tree-lined driveway as they approached the house. It was a stately, two-storey mansion, and all the outside lights were on, showing up the beautiful iron lacework that decorated the traditional colonial verandas.

Ann wondered if the lights were a gesture of welcome home to the master of the house, or if they were automatically switched on every night. Other lights around the garden displayed some magnificent pine trees and banks of azaleas. It was certainly an impressive sight.

There were other buildings beyond the house, some large, some small, and seemingly set in a semicircle. Ann thought of barns and stables, and perhaps staff quarters. She knew racehorses were bred here. However, Matthew Fielding didn't bother identifying anything for her, and Ann didn't ask.

He drove around the back of the house to a set of garages and parked his Porsche in one of them. Conscious of not antagonising him unnecessarily, Ann waited for him to open her passenger door and thanked him as she climbed out. He collected his attaché case and her suitcase. They walked across a huge paved courtyard. A well-lit path, edged with massed pansies and primulas, led to the house.

One of the front doors opened before they reached it. A tall, spare, grey-haired woman beamed a welcome at them. She was dressed in a smart tartan skirt and green cardigan, and her face looked remarkably young for her sixty-odd years.

'Matt . . . you made good time,' she commented, with obvious pleasure at seeing him.

'Friday evening traffic is always a curse,' he growled, then smiled affectionately at her. 'You look well, Mother.'

'I'm always well,' she laughed, and looked curiously at Ann.

'This is Carmody,' her son introduced offhandedly.

'Hello, Mrs Mallory,' Ann smiled, offering her hand.

It was taken and gently squeezed. 'Hello, my dear.' She threw a chagrined look at her son. 'I assume you do have a first name?'

'It's Ann.'

The older woman smiled. 'Well, that's something, at least. Now, come inside out of the cold, and I'll show you to your room.'

They entered a spacious foyer. An archway on one side opened into a very elegant living-room, where a log fire cheered a magnificent marble fire-place. Mrs Mallory led Ann to the staircase in the opposite direction and chatted pleasantly as they walked up.

'I know Matt will keep you closeted in the study most of the time, but please feel free to wander anywhere you like when he's not slave-driving. I've put some magazines in your room in case you like reading when you go to bed, and if there's anything else you fancy, please say so.'

'I'll be fine,' Ann said warmly, liking the mother a lot better than she liked the son.

She was shown to a beautiful room. The four-poster bed had a magnificent patchwork quilt, and all the furniture was in the antique class. And, to Ann's relief and pleasure, there was an en suite bathroom, its feature tiles cleverly echoing the patchwork pattern in the bedroom.

'It's all lovely,' she enthused. 'Thank you.'

Mrs Mallory smiled. 'There has to be some compensation for working for my son. I know how demanding he is. On himself, as well as everyone around him. I had to virtually blackmail him to come home this weekend. I hope it hasn't put you out too much, dear.'

'No. Not at all. Besides, the job comes first,' Ann said matter-of-factly.

The older woman looked at her in a slightly puzzled fashion, then shook her head. 'Come down when you're ready, dear. Dinner will be in half an hour.'

Apparently Mrs Mallory didn't understand career-women, Ann thought bemusedly, but the more she thought about it, the more sense it made. Matthew Fielding's mother had married twice, and her son's attitude to women had to have some roots in his relationship with his mother. Ann recalled his earlier comment—women needed looking after—and no doubt his wealth cushioned his mother's life, even if he didn't personally stand guard for her.

He had dropped Ann's suitcase just inside the door of her room, and she unpacked her things before going downstairs again. Mother and son were sitting by the fire in the living-room, obviously enjoying each other's company. Ann hesitated at the archway, but she had left it as late as she courteously could to join them. It was only five minutes short of the half-hour Mrs Mallory had specified.

Matthew Fielding spotted her and rose to his feet. 'Don't hang there, Carmody. Come and sit down. And what would you like to drink? A sherry——'

'No, nothing, thank you,' Ann quickly declined.

'It's time for us to go into the dining-room, anyway,' his mother announced, and moved to draw Ann along with her.

They sat at one end of a table which would easily seat ten. Again the furniture was all polished antiques: rich, gleaming, and elegantly styled. Matthew Fielding opened a bottle of white wine and looked irritated when Ann refused a glass.

'I told you we're not working tonight, Carmody,' he said sharply. 'You can relax.'

'I don't mean to offend, Mr Fielding. The fact is, I never drink any form of alcohol,' Ann stated quietly.

He frowned at her disbelievingly, but his mother instantly saved any awkwardness. 'What soft drink would you like, Ann? Or perhaps some fruit juice?'

Ann smiled her gratitude. 'I'm not fussy, Mrs Mallory. Some lemonade, or——'

'Say no more.'

The conversation was interrupted by the arrival of soup, carried in by a homely woman of late middle-age.

'Oh, thank you, Rene,' Mrs Mallory said warmly. 'And could you bring some lemonade for Miss Carmody? Ann, this is Rene Thayer. She and her husband, Bill, look after everything about the house.'

Polite pleasantries were exchanged, the lemonade was brought, and they started on the first course. It was a creamy pumpkin soup which Ann thoroughly enjoyed. Rene Thayer cleared away the emptied plates and glowed under Matthew Fielding's compliments.

'I know it's your favourite,' she said. 'You should come home more often, Mr Fielding. No food like good home-cooking.'

Ann could not help thinking how very attractive he looked when he smiled with good humour. The brown eyes sparkled warmly, and his face had a softer, kinder look. But then he wasn't out to win anything in this house. It was all his. The king of the castle could afford to be benevolent.

'Where does your family live, Ann?' his mother enquired with polite interest.

It was an ordinary enough question, but Ann was aware of Matthew Fielding's gaze on her, waiting to dissect her answer and file it away in his computer mind for possible future ammunition. He had the ability to manipulate any knowledge to his advantage.

She answered reluctantly. 'I have no immediate family, Mrs Mallory.'

'An orphan?' Matthew Fielding quizzed.

He was not going to leave the subject alone now it had been raised. His curiosity was aroused. The best thing to do was give a matter-of-fact account that gave him no colour to play with.

She shrugged. 'Not in the sense you mean. My father died when I was a child. He was an immigrant from England. I do have relatives over there, but for obvious reasons of distance, we're not close. My mother was an orphan. Brought up in foster-homes. So I have no family on her side. She died a few years ago.'

The bare bones neatly evaded filling in her real background: her father's alcoholism, that had changed his moods from ebullient gaiety to black fury from day to day; her mother's need for love, which had permeated both her private and public life; the high-low years of never knowing what she would come home to.

Mrs Mallory shook her head sympathetically. 'It must be very lonely for you. I suppose that's why you've taken on such a time-consuming job.'

Ann could not help a little smile at the justification Mrs Mallory had come up with, but before she could form a tactful reply Matthew Fielding laughed.

'Don't believe it, Mother. Carmody eats it.'

'Eats what?' his mother asked, puzzled.

'Work. She gobbles up everything I throw at her, and thrives on it.' His eyes twinkled at her. 'Isn't that the truth, Carmody?'

For a moment there was a sharp flash of understanding between them—like recognising like—and Ann's heart squeezed tight. She wrenched her eyes from his and fastened them on his mother. 'I enjoy work, Mrs Mallory,' she said flatly.

'But . . . you must have other interests,' the older woman persisted.

Ann was saved from answering by the arrival of the main course—roast beef and beautifully cooked fresh vegetables. She didn't want to talk about herself. It was dangerous ground—too easy to slip into tell-tale bits of the past. She had to keep remembering that this was a work situation, not a social one.

Before Mrs Mallory could pick up on the conversation again, Ann deliberately took the initiative, asking her about her interests and how she filled in her life at Fernlea.

The breeding programme with the horses, and the seasonal changes made to the garden, took her through until dessert—a delicious apple pie with cream—and various trips overseas finished off the after-dinner coffee. Ann rose from the table to excuse herself for the night, well aware that Matthew Fielding had watched her tactics with silent amusement.

'Oh, must you go? I've so enjoyed our chat,' Mrs Mallory protested.

'I'm afraid I must. I'm very tired,' Ann said firmly. 'Thank you for a lovely dinner. It's been delightful talking to you, Mrs Mallory.' She directed a nod somewhere in between her host and hostess. 'Goodnight.'

'Breakfast at eight, Carmody,' Matthew Fielding called after her.

'I'll be ready, sir,' Ann replied, and made good her escape.

She still felt shaken by that jolt of attraction that had hit her at the dinner-table. It wasn't simply that Matthew Fielding was good-looking. She could deal with that. But she did not care to feel any intimate mind-locking with him. It was wrong. It was dangerous. She had to keep her distance, because any emotional involvement with him could only bring her grief. She didn't want to lose her job now. The work was more challenging and satisfying than all her previous work experiences.

Besides, he would never really recognise her as an equal. He was a male chauvinist through and through. No chance of happy accord with him! It was utterly stupid to feel attracted to him in any shape or form.

But Ann received yet another even less welcome jolt the next morning. Despite the luxurious comfort of the four-poster bed, she had not slept well. She rose early and dressed, thinking she might go for a walk before breakfast. But then she stepped out on the veranda outside her bedroom, and the beauty of the view drew her to the railing.

The sun was rising and the sky was streaked with pastels. A morning mist wreathed the green pastures beyond the gardens. Ann was entranced. Impossible to see anything like this in the city. And the air was wonderfully fresh—sharp and invigorating. There was no noise at all except for the twitter of birds. Until she heard a loud splash of water below her.

She looked down to the swimming-pool that had been cleverly set into the landscape, and there was Matthew Fielding ploughing up and down its length. She had known he was a fitness fanatic, but not to the extent of swimming in an outdoor pool on a cold winter's morning.

She watched him in silent bemusement. He was a strong swimmer. He carved through lap after lap without any lagging of energy. He did not look tired, even when he stopped. He hauled himself out of the water and snatched up a towel to give himself a brisk rub-down. Ann's stomach gave a peculiar lurch.

She had noticed the powerfully muscled arms cleaving through the water, but hadn't realised that the rest of him would be in such perfect proportion. His shoulders were broad and strong. His back rippled with superb muscular tone. His waist was firm and lean. His bottom, only barely covered by a pair of brief black swimming-trunks, was taut and neat. And his legs were aggressively masculine—strong, muscular, firmly fleshed.

He picked up a thick bathrobe and turned around as he thrust his arms into it. He wasn't really hairy at all. A sprinkle of black curls clung high on his chest, and the rest of him was smooth, gleaming skin. To Ann's intense mortification he glanced up and caught her staring at him.

'Good morning!' he called. 'If you'd like a swim, Carmody, there are some spare suits in the cabana.'

She found her voice with some difficulty. 'No, thank you. It's too cold for me.'

'The pool's heated.'

'No, thanks all the same.'

She retreated swiftly to her bedroom and stayed there until breakfast-time, shocked that Matthew Fielding's body should have fascinated her so much. She had the awful feeling that she would never see him again without picturing what he was like under his clothes. It did no good at all telling herself he was just a healthy male in superb condition. She had reacted to him physically... sexually. And that was very, very disturbing.

Nevertheless, there was no running away from him, and at precisely eight o'clock Ann steeled herself to join him in the breakfast-room. To her enormous relief, his head was in the morning newspaper and he only glanced up to give her a quick greeting.

'The *Herald* is there if you want to read it,' he said.

She poured herself a glass of orange juice from a jug set on the table, and glanced at the headlines. Mrs Thayer came in with plates of bacon and eggs and freshly toasted bread. Ann exchanged greetings with her as she set everything down. Matthew Fielding put the newspaper aside and addressed himself to his breakfast.

'Sleep well, Carmody?'

'Yes, thank you.'

'Early riser?'

'Sometimes.'

His eyes danced at her. 'Remind me to use your talent for drawing people out, Carmody. Of course, my mother is easily led, but you were smooth. Very smooth.'

She concentrated on buttering a piece of toast. 'I found your mother's talk interesting, Mr Fielding,' she said warily.

'Mmm...' He ate a few mouthfuls before addressing her again. 'Most people like to talk about themselves. Why don't you, Carmody?'

She was ready for that one. 'I didn't think it was my place, sir.'

He gave a low soft laugh. 'Little Miss Perfect.'

Her pulse leapt in a totally disruptive manner, and Ann concentrated fiercely on her breakfast, trying her utmost to ignore the man sitting opposite her.

'What are your interests?' he asked bluntly. 'You can skip work, younger men and exotic clothes.'

She raised cool blue eyes. 'My other interests are not relevant to the job, sir.'

Brown eyes stabbed into hers. 'Let's say I'm interested in finding out.'

She swiftly dropped her lashes, veiling the mad inner turmoil his words stirred. She went on eating, not rising to his dubious suggestion.

'Carmody, you haven't answered.'

'No, sir.'

'Well?' he persisted.

Ann got herself under control and flicked him a derisive look. 'You want the truth, sir?'

'It would be enlightening.'

Ann put down her knife and fork and forced herself to look him straight in the face. 'You like to win. You're not interested in me. Not as a person. The only reason you want to know is so you can use the information against me if it suits you. Possible ammunition. Grist to your mill. You simply like to win, Mr Fielding.'

He looked startled for a moment, then he threw back his head and laughed. 'So do you, Carmody. So do you. We're two of a kind.'

He was still grinning as he pushed himself back from the table and stood up. He exuded a vitality that dimmed the memory of every man Ann had ever met. Life was suddenly full of yawning pitfalls.

'We can have coffee in the study,' he said, anticipation sparkling in his eyes. 'Let's get to work, Carmody.'

It was easier to cast Matthew Fielding back in his proper place while they worked. But still Ann felt tense and agitated whenever he came to look over her shoulder at her progress on one item or another. They didn't stop for lunch. Mrs Thayer brought them in a plate of sandwiches. Coffee was delivered at frequent intervals. A halt was finally called at four o'clock.

'Enough, Carmody. Go and have a rest. My sister will be arriving soon. We'll expect you in the lounge at six-thirty.'

She nodded and left, relieved to have the hours off in order to compose herself for the evening onslaught of Matthew Fielding's company. She hadn't seen his mother all day, but Ann hoped that Mrs Mallory might once again provide a defence against her son's discomfiting presence.

She wished now that she hadn't risen to his challenge on the exotic clothes issue. The cheongsam was inevitably going to draw attention to herself. She wondered if she could get away with wearing the grey suit, then decided that she would be only asking for more trouble if she flouted his instructions.

Feeling decidedly depressed with herself and the situation, Ann undressed, pulled on the dragon housecoat and lay down on the bed, trying hard to relax. It was no use. Thoughts kept tumbling through her mind—thoughts she did not want to examine at all. She reached for the magazines Mrs Mallory had provided and flipped through them. Nothing held her attention. She wished she could play her music. It was the best way she knew of lifting her spirits. She could lose herself in music.

Restless with inactivity, she got up, took a shower and washed her hair. Blow-drying the silky fineness into a smooth shape took up some time. Since she was wearing the cheongsam, Ann couldn't see much point in not going the whole hog, so she exchanged her glasses for contact lenses and made up her eyes—shadow, liner and mascara all lending a subtle emphasis.

She drew on extra-fine tights, all too aware of the thigh-high slits in her dress. Matthew Fielding had only ever seen her in the all-disguising grey suits. His eyes were probably going to pop out. And suddenly that thought gave Ann a lot of satisfaction. He had disturbed her with his body. She wanted to give him a dose of the same treatment.

The cheongsam fitted her curves like a second skin—a silk-brocade skin that shimmered as she moved. The rich blue material was the same shade as her eyes, and gold thread picked out the brocade pattern in a rough V from her shoulders to her waist. It also formed a rich border around the hem and the side-slits, as well as edging the long, elegant sleeves. The high Chinese collar suited Ann's long neck, and dispensed with any need for jewellery. Her hair gleamed golden above it, and the short style with its fringe was perfect for the dress.

Ann slid her feet into high-heeled gold sandals, which consisted of very thin, elegant heels and only two cleverly positioned straps. She surveyed the full effect in the mirror. Exotic he wanted to see, and exotic she looked. No doubt about it.

At precisely six-thirty she walked along the hallway to the staircase, ready to descend. She could hear voices below—adults' and children's. Matthew Fielding's sister and her brood had definitely arrived. Mindful that she was about to make an entrance that would probably kill all conversation, Ann straightened her shoulders, tilted her chin high and took the stairs very carefully, terrified that she might topple on her high heels.

She was half-way down when Matthew Fielding glanced up and saw her through the archway. He was moving towards the cocktail cabinet, perhaps checking to see if she was on her way to join the family. He was a stickler for punctuality.

He stopped dead in his tracks and stared, a totally incredulous look on his face. He muttered something indistinguishable, but it was enough to break the general chatter. He started forward jerkily, then moved with quick fluidity to the foot of the stairs in the foyer.

Ann felt a wild surge of triumph as his gaze ran up and down her tightly sheathed body. There was no finesse about the way his eyes lurched from the full thrust of her breasts, the narrow cinched-in waist, the rounded swell of her hips, the long, lissom curves of her legs, and back again in a distracted zigzag fashion until they finally dragged themselves up to her face.

'Where are your glasses?' he croaked, as if he had to cling to something familiar.

'I wear contact lenses when I'm dressed up, Mr Fielding,' she said, with truly marvellous composure. She was singing inside, the most exultant arias in the whole history of music.

'Carmody...' He swallowed. 'You sure as hell like to win.'

'I hope I'm not too out of taste,' she said, rubbing it in with inner glee.

He was wearing one of his plain white shirts, a quiet, tasteful tie, and a conservative navy-blue suit. He shook his head. 'Somehow, I think my family is about to be too dazzled to think about it,' he said ruefully.

He offered his arm with mocking courtesy as she took the last step on to the foyer. 'Are you sure you want to be seen with me, Mr Fielding?' she asked, feigning uncertainty. 'I could go back and put my grey suit on.'

He grinned. 'Carmody, enough is enough! I asked for it. You've socked it to me. I'll live with it. Though I have a terrible suspicion it isn't going to be easy.'

She took his arm and he led her into the lounge.

Everyone stared at her, even the children—two little boys of about two and four years of age, and a baby girl sitting on Mrs Mallory's lap—a lap that was clothed in a dark red silk which formed a very classy dress. A young man of about thirty rose slowly to his feet. He seemed to have trouble keeping his jaw from dropping open. He wore a grey, conservative suit. A woman in her mid-twenties, dressed in a lovely green velvet dinner-gown, stood by the fireplace, her eyes rounding in surprise.

Matthew Fielding gestured towards her. 'My sister, Ellie Sanders. Her husband, Brian. And children in order of age—Jason, Kyle and Leonie. And I'd like you all to meet Carmody, who goes by the name of Ann,' he rolled off with cheerful aplomb, showing not the slightest embarrassment in her wildly overdressed appearance.

'No, not Ann!' Ellie Sanders burst out, shaking her head in emphatic denial. 'There can't be two people named Carmody with that face and hair. Your name is Angel, isn't it? Angel Carmody. I remember you too well to be mistaken.'

CHAPTER FIVE

ANN froze.

It wasn't so much the unexpectedness of the recognition, but the horror of realising that, if Ellie Sanders knew that much about her, the link with her mother was also known. And it would all come out. In front of Matthew Fielding!

No more secrets.

No wall of privacy to keep him locked out.

Her life was about to be stripped naked of all the cover she had constructed since her mother's death.

Her arm was still resting on his. She was unaware of her nails clawing up his coat-sleeve to curl painfully into her palm. Her gaze was fixed on Ellie Sanders, as helplessly fixed as if the woman were a cobra about to strike.

Matthew Fielding's sister had a head full of bouncy black curls that were bobbing around in excitement. Her dark eyes glistened with certainty. Her red mouth quivered from the pressure of a fountain of words ready to burst into speech.

How could she shut the woman up? The question shrieked across Ann's mind. But now, in the hour of her greatest need, her sharp mind was appallingly sluggish in coming up with an answer.

73

And Ellie Sanders was too impatient to wait for one. 'You must remember, Mother,' she urged, any sense of discretion tossed to the winds as she bubbled forth. 'Who could forget Angel Carmody singing at her last concert at Rose Bay? You could have heard a pin drop in that hall during the "Ave Maria".'

She looked admiringly at Ann. 'It was so beautiful, it sent shivers up my spine.'

Mrs Mallory looked at Ann too, in wondering reappraisal. 'Yes. I thought there was something familiar about your face last night. But I couldn't place it. Your voice should have jolted my memory. That pure bell-like tone——'

'But what on earth are you doing . . . working for Matt?' Ellie blurted out, again shaking the mass of black curls, her eyes asking more in her frank puzzlement.

Every word had felt like a block of wood, hitting Ann over the head. But she had to stop Ellie Sanders in her tracks, no matter what effort it took. Desperate to alter the direction of the conversation, she forced herself to speak.

'I'm afraid you have the advantage of me, Mrs Sanders. I have no recollection of meeting either you or Mrs Mallory before this weekend. And I'm sure Mr Fielding has explained to you my position in his company. I regret that it was necessary for me to intrude on your birthday party tonight. Please . . . don't let me interrupt your family pleasure.'

She was unaware of the hunted appeal in her eyes as she glanced up at Matthew Fielding. 'If I may sit down, sir, you can go on with whatever you were doing before you so kindly escorted me in.'

There was a dreadful silence as he led her to a chair. Ann almost collapsed into it, only her innate pride dictating that she not appear as rattled as she felt.

'Lemonade, Carmody?' Matthew Fielding murmured. 'I remember you don't drink the heavy stuff.'

She could not, would not look at him. He sounded sympathetic, but that couldn't be right. He was simply keeping quiet, avidly waiting for more revelations.

'Yes, please,' she said, hoping it would take him out of the room. Not that it would do any good. He could pump his sister any time he liked.

Ellie Sanders pounced again. 'I can't understand it! I know I'm not mistaken! Oh, I realise you wouldn't remember me. I was a junior at school when you were a senior. But, of course, we all knew Angel Carmody. You made it such a pleasure to go to church, just to hear you lead the choir.'

The words weren't blocks of wood this time. They were nails in her coffin, leaving no leeway for escape! And Matthew Fielding didn't leave the room. There was a jug of iced lemonade all ready for her on the cocktail cabinet.

For one wild moment Ann wondered if she could get away with denying her identity, but common sense told her the facts could too easily be checked. She had been educated at the convent at Rose Bay. It was one of the more exclusive private schools in Sydney. Her mother had insisted on it. Only the best for her daughter. And her photograph was featured in the school magazine every year she had been there—and some of those years had obviously been shared by Ellie Sanders!

Minimise the damage—it was the only route open to her now. 'That was a long time ago,' she said quietly.

'But pushing paper for Matt!' Ellie said in critical disbelief. 'How could you be satisfied with that? It's such a shocking waste of your talent.'

Ellie Sanders was like a dog with a bone. She gnawed away, giving Ann no opportunity to answer. 'How could you not go on with it, Angel? A voice like yours! What happened to you to make you give it up?'

At last she paused.

'Perhaps you were...too impressionable... when you were a junior, Mrs Sanders,' Ann suggested pointedly, fiercely willing her to let the subject drop. 'You must have thought my voice better than it was.'

'Ellie...' Matthew Fielding slid into the treacherous impasse. 'Whatever you thought of Carmody's ability to sing, I can assure you that it was only one of many talents. Do you really think I would hire any hack to be my personal assistant?' he demanded drily.

He handed Ann her lemonade, his eyes twinkling down at her in mocking amusement before sweeping back to his family. 'Of course, she can sing. Carmody can do anything I ask her to do.'

She clutched the glass tightly. She had never thought she would ever be grateful to Matthew Fielding for anything, but, even if it was only his ego prompting a protest, she could have hugged him for his support.

But then Ann's gaze fell on Ellie's husband. The look on his face froze the gratitude out of her veins. Brian Sanders was appraising her as if he had little doubt about the talent she had been hired for. His gaze was travelling around the high glimpse of thigh afforded by the slit in her dress. A knowing little quirk curled his lips.

Mrs Mallory picked that moment to support her daughter. 'Matt...you don't know. You never came to Ellie's school concerts. Ann...Angel...sang like one. If you had heard her, you would never forget.'

'That's very flattering of you, Mrs Mallory,' Ann almost snapped, infuriated by Brian's snide assumption. 'But Mr Fielding is right. Endless rehearsals would have bored me. Nothing happened...' she shot an icy, quelling look at the daughter '...to make me give it up. I simply chose to follow a different career. I happen to prefer the more mentally stimulating arena of the business world.'

Ellie Sanders stared back at her, still disbelieving.

Mrs Mallory shook her head. 'It seems such a shame...'

But Ann had recovered from her initial shock. And she didn't give a damn what Brian Sanders thought. She knew the truth. She was the only one in this room who knew the whole truth. They could speculate as much as they liked, but, as far as she was concerned, it was none of their business! And that was the end of the matter.

She took firm control, determined not to fall victim to any more personal questions. 'You must have married very young, Mrs Sanders,' she said, her gaze pointedly sweeping around the three children.

Ellie laughed. 'Almost straight out of school. And do call me Ellie.' She moved to sit on the arm-rest of her husband's chair, and smiled fondly at him. 'I fell in love with Brian when I was sixteen. He was twenty-two at the time, and thought I was a precocious brat.'

'Not true,' he grinned up at her. 'But you were very young. Although you sure made it hellishly difficult for me to keep my hands off you.'

The older boy, Jason, suddenly plucked up the courage to approach Ann. 'Why haven't you got black hair? I've seen pictures of Chinese girls, and they always have black hair.'

Ann was given the opening she had been waiting for. From then on she deftly focused all the attention on the children, until Ellie announced it was their bedtime. Mrs Mallory carried the baby, Brian picked up the two-year-old, and Ellie took Jason's hand to lead him upstairs. Their exodus left Ann alone with Matthew Fielding.

He strolled over to the fireplace, propped his elbow on the mantel, and surveyed her with a mixture of admiration and amusement. Her mind shrieked caution, even as her pulse quickened and every nerve in her body seemed to vibrate with awareness.

'Angel?' he drawled quizzically.

'I didn't choose the name, Mr Fielding, any more than you chose yours,' she retorted, projecting a dry boredom into her voice.

'True. But most people don't bother changing their name.'

She sighed. Impatiently. 'Mr Fielding, if you had been called Gabriel, wouldn't you have shortened it to Gabe once you were out from under your family's wing?'

He grinned. 'Point taken.'

Ann's heart performed a double loop. She could appreciate now why he was such a lady-killer. When he grinned like that, with his eyes as well as the charming flash of teeth, his strong, male sex appeal took a mega-leap.

'On the other hand,' he continued, 'I doubt that I would react quite so intensely if someone faced me with Gabriel. Irritated, perhaps, but...' the sparkle in his eyes fused into sharp laser beams, probing for vulnerability '...but I rather fancy it was the connection to singing that upset you.'

Ann silently cursed his shrewd perception, even as she stretched her mouth into a mocking smile. 'I find the connection tiresome, Mr Fielding. As tiresome as you bringing it up again now. My life has moved on.'

He was not bluffed. 'You're hiding something, Carmody,' he said quietly. 'Just as you've been hiding your delectable body under those iniquitous grey suits.'

'You didn't hire a body, sir,' Ann reminded him icily. 'Nor a voice. I don't want either to become involved in our business together, any more than you want your body or your voice to have any bearing on our working relationship.'

Their eyes locked. Far from defusing the situation, Ann's challenge sparked off an explosive tension between them. She knew—it was written in his eyes—that he wanted nothing better at that moment than to drag her off and force her to surrender everything to him.

Perhaps that was imbued in the nature of men like Matthew Fielding—the want...no, the need...to dominate everything around them. And Ann found herself responding to that look with an equally fierce need to fight him all the way. If Matthew Fielding ever tried to take her—as he was envisaging right now—she would do her utmost to enslave him so totally that he would never look at another woman again.

'Well...'

The soft, breathy word dropped into the silence like a bombshell, startling both of them. Mrs Mallory stood in the archway, her gaze darting from Ann to her son and back again. What she saw seemed to delight her. Her eyes were alight with pleasurable speculation.

'Well, what, Mother?' Matthew Fielding snapped at her, clearly not in full control of himself.

'Nothing! Nothing, really,' Mrs Mallory rushed out, instinctively soothing. 'I was just thinking how lovely Ann looks. So few people really dress up these days, and I always think it's such a pity! It's the cost of labour, of course. It makes everything so expensive. But when I was a girl, all our evening-gowns were beaded or sequinned or threaded with silver or gold.'

She smiled indulgently at Ann as she walked in and sat down. 'Women really enjoyed being women back then,' she enthused. 'Men pandered to them——'

'Carmody doesn't like men pandering to her, Mother,' Matthew Fielding put in drily. 'Anyone who tried it would probably get his head bitten off. She even likes to carry her own suitcases.'

His mother looked taken aback.

Her son smiled sardonically. 'Don't be fooled by the dress. Carmody simply has a personal taste for the exotic.'

Ellie and Brian Sanders made their reappearance on this line, and Ellie picked up on the end of it. 'Only to be expected,' she laughed. 'The highlight

of visiting-days at school was when Angel
Carmody's mother swept in to take her off. She
always had our eyes hanging out on stalks. Even
the nuns couldn't resist! She gave another di-
mension to the meaning of the word "glamour".'

Ann's heart squirmed with anxiety. How on earth
could she stop Ellie from babbling on?

It was Brian who did the damage before Ann
could even open her mouth. 'Ellie was just telling
me that your mother is Chantelle. No wonder
you've got a good singing voice.'

'What's your mother doing now, Angel?' Ellie
demanded curiously. 'I haven't heard of her for
quite some time.'

'Ellie . . .' Mrs Mallory frowned warningly at her
daughter and glanced sympathetically at Ann.

'My mother died a few years ago,' Ann stated
baldly. There was nothing else to do. And Matthew
Fielding knew it all now.

Chantelle! Her mother's surname had never been
used. Chantelle—sensational in life, and even more
sensational in death! There would hardly be one
Australian who didn't recognise the name. Top-line
singer . . . star of theatre and television . . . with a
penchant for young lovers and outrageous state-
ments that were always titillating fodder for the
media. But nothing more scandalously titillating
than the manner of her death.

'Died?' Ellie echoed dazedly. 'But . . . she wasn't
old or . . .'

'You were overseas with Brian at the time, Ellie,' Matthew Fielding cut in peremptorily. 'It was an accident. Let's leave it at that, shall we?' he added in a soft voice that held a core of steel.

He knew, Ann thought wretchedly. Anyone who read newspapers as assiduously as Matthew Fielding did would certainly recall that juicy scandal! It had carried headlines for weeks, particularly with the inquiry that had followed Chantelle's death.

'I forgot to tell you about the pups, Ellie,' Mrs Mallory rushed in with almost desperate tact. 'They were born this morning. Five of them...'

Ann sipped her lemonade. Her throat felt like a parched desert. She didn't have to look at Matthew Fielding to know what he was remembering... and thinking.

Chantelle, found dead from an overdose of drugs, naked, with two young men who had died with her—members of the band who had played for her. Ann didn't want to remember the details. They had been experimenting with a new designer drug which shouldn't have killed. It was supposed to give the user a release from inhibitions. Only someone, somewhere, had made a fatal mistake with the strength of the fix.

If Ann had even suspected for a moment that Matthew Fielding would discover who her mother had been, she would never have used that dreadfully evocative line about preferring younger men. Like mother, like daughter, he would be thinking. Just like Roger Hopman.

And her dress tonight would reinforce the image.

Yet none of it had any real meaning. In one way her mother had remained far more innocent than Ann, although no one would ever believe it.

Mrs Thayer announced dinner.

Ann rose and walked into the dining-room with the others, but she wasn't really with them. Not even Matthew Fielding's presence could penetrate the wall of reserve she had drawn around her. The wall shut him out more than anyone else.

She sat down. She spoke when spoken to. She was vaguely aware that the conversation had moved from dogs to horses, but she didn't follow the sense of it. She ate mechanically, one course after another. Eventually they moved back to the lounge, where Matthew Fielding opened yet another bottle of champagne and toasted Ellie's birthday. Ann pasted a smile on her face and politely echoed the toast.

She felt like a ghost at the feast. A vanishing act was almost in order. Another ten minutes or so, she calculated.

'I've had a lovely birthday,' Ellie bubbled. 'There's only one more thing that could make it really special...'

She looked at Ann with bright anticipation. Ann stared back blankly, not realising that something was expected from her. Her mind was already reaching for the privacy of her room.

'I know it's a lot to ask...' Ellie was smiling at her, hands joined in prayerful appeal '...but if you'd just sing one song for us, Angel. For me?'

'Ellie!' her mother whipped in reproachfully. 'That's not fair. In any event, we can't provide any appropriate accompaniment.'

'Angel never needed any accompaniment, Mother,' Ellie argued. 'She has perfect pitch.'

Her eyes swung back to Ann, hopeful and eager for her request to be granted.

The idea was total anathema to Ann. 'I'm sorry. I can't,' she said bluntly.

'Be reasonable, Ellie,' Matthew Fielding drawled. 'You're referring back to ten years ago. And Carmody has satisfied herself with other activities since then.'

The derisive tone of his voice jarred on Ann's ears. Her eyes stabbed at him. His mocking look defined the 'other activities' he had in mind—sex, drugs, debauchery. All too predictable, Ann thought, and promptly hated him for it.

No matter that she had given him reason to think what he did. He wasn't only thinking badly of her; he was thinking contemptuously of her mother. And he had no right. No right at all! He was the kind of man who would have used her mother, without ever valuing the real person inside.

'You assume too much, Mr Fielding,' she said, her voice so cold and clipped that it instantly gave rise to an awkward tension in the room. She rose to her feet with almost bristling hauteur and looked down at Ellie. 'One song.'

No one said a word as Ann walked to the archway at the end of the room. When she turned around every face was lifted to her, wondering, not knowing what to expect, but waiting for it to happen.

Ann directed a twisted smile at Ellie. 'Birthday or not, I do not sing this for you.' Her gaze flicked to Matthew Fielding, hard and bitter. 'It's for my mother, whose gift it was.'

She took a deep breath, and without the slightest falter released the voice that still had the power to mesmerise with its pure, tonal quality. She sang the 'Ave Maria' which her mother had always liked best, and into every note she poured the devotion that no one else would ever understand.

Then, when the song was finished, she said, 'Goodnight,' and walked away. The silence she left behind her was unbroken. The only noise was the soft thud of her shoes on each step. At last she reached her room, and the solid cedar door closed between her and Matthew Fielding's family.

CHAPTER SIX

MAYBE it was some defence mechanism, or maybe the stress of the evening had deadened Ann's mind. Whatever the reason, almost as soon as she climbed into bed, she sank into a deep, heavy sleep.

It was seven-thirty when she woke the next morning. Matthew Fielding had not stipulated a time for breakfast, or when they were to start work in the study, but Ann did not want him knocking on her door. She wanted no familiarity from him at all. If he dared to bring up any facet of what he had learnt last night, she would cut him dead!

She pushed herself out of bed, had a quick shower, and dressed in her grey suit. No make-up. Her owl-framed glasses replaced the contact lenses. Her hair received a perfunctory brush. She donned her walking shoes. If breakfast was to be later than the eight o'clock of yesterday, she would get out of the house for a while.

Ann had no idea if the Sanders family had stayed overnight, but the only person she found downstairs was Rene Thayer in the kitchen.

'Did Mr Fielding say what time he wanted breakfast, Mrs Thayer?' Ann enquired.

'Always nine o'clock on Sunday. But if you'd like some now, Miss Carmody...'

'No. No, thank you. I wondered how much time I had, that's all. I'd like to go for a walk.'

'As you like,' was the good-natured reply.

Ann did not linger around the landscaped gardens, or head towards the stables. She did not want to meet or talk with anyone. She followed the driveway to the entrance gates of the property, pausing now and then to admire the horses that were being put out in the lushly pastured paddocks.

On the way back she leant on the fence near a large dam. A flock of wild ducks were sailing around the wide expanse of water. It was peaceful and pleasant watching their antics—until she inadvertently glanced up at the house and saw *him watching her*.

He was at the railing of the upper-storey veranda, just as she had been yesterday morning. Perhaps he had seen her head lift and realised she had caught sight of him. Whatever the reason, she had no sooner spotted him than he jerked away and re-entered his room, closing the door behind him.

Which was fine by Ann! She didn't want Matthew Fielding watching her. He could keep his eyes elsewhere! She didn't even want him looking at her unless it was absolutely necessary.

She had known from the start that this weekend boded no good for her, but not even her trusty intuition had warned just how bad it would be. However, Matthew Fielding needn't start thinking that his knowledge of her background gave him any advantage over her. If he made any reference to it, any reference at all, she would make him pay for it, one way or another.

Ann glanced at her watch. It was eight-forty. Time for her to be getting back to the house. She paced her return to the last minute.

Matthew Fielding was seated at the breakfast-table. Alone. He was perusing one of the Sunday newspapers.

'Good morning,' Ann said with cool aplomb.

'Carmody.' He nodded, his eyes as hard as hers as he rose to see her seated. The back of her neck prickled as he pushed in her chair.

'Enjoy your walk?' he asked.

'Yes, thank you.'

She picked up the second newspaper which was lying on the table, and glued her eyes to the front-page articles.

Breakfast was served. Neither Matthew Fielding nor Ann initiated any further conversation. On his instruction, they retired to the study, where Mrs Thayer brought them coffee. As soon as they were alone, without threat of interruption, the brown eyes bored into Ann's, too purposeful for her to do anything but block his scrutiny with clear blue ice.

'I'm sorry you were embarrassed last night. That was not my intention, Carmody.'

'Shall we get on with the job, sir? That *is* why you asked me here,' Ann said pointedly.

He picked up an envelope from his desk and held it out to her. 'My mother spoke to Ellie after you retired last night. My sister was most anxious you read this note from her first thing this morning. I would be obliged if you did so.'

Ann took the envelope, sensing he was determined to push it on her if necessary. She opened it, extracted the note, and read it, not allowing one word of it to impinge upon her fixed composure.

Dear Ann,

Please believe that the last thing I would have wanted was to distress you. I'm so sorry for having recalled what must have been a very painful time for you. I admired your mother very much. And, while it might sound very silly to you, I hero-worshipped Angel Carmody at school, which I hope explains my tactless reactions last night. Explains, but hardly excuses. Please forgive me. I am not usually so stupid, and if we ever meet again I promise you it will be on your terms, and I will never refer to the past again.

Yours sincerely,
Ellie Sanders

It was a kind and generous apology, and Ann forgave the girl on the spot. She refolded the note, tucked it in its envelope, and slipped it into her jacket pocket.

She raised her gaze to Matthew Fielding again. He stared back at her—hard. There was a heart-twisting need, almost a hunger in his eyes. She could feel him willing her to comment, perhaps even to explain the past, justify her behaviour in some way. Certainly he wanted something from her. And for one weak moment Ann ached for him to understand.

But she was foolish for wishing he was capable of it...a man like him, who used women for his pleasure! And hadn't he said he wanted no female emotionalism around him? Pride forbade her showing any vulnerability to his opinion.

'I have obliged you, sir,' she stated evenly. 'What work would you like me to start on?'

His mouth thinned. His eyes blazed with angry frustration. He reached for a bundle of papers and slammed them on the desk in front of her. 'Check the figures on those quotations, and point out anything you think I should know about.'

It was a flattering deference to her judgement, but Ann had already shown her worth to him in this kind of meticulous checking, so she felt no pleasure in his instruction. She simply concentrated on doing as he asked. They worked until one o'clock, when Matthew Fielding abruptly announced that he was satisfied with what they had achieved, and began to pack up all his papers.

'Lunch on the patio in fifteen minutes. We'll head back to Sydney after that.'

Apparently Ellie's family had not stayed overnight. Only Mrs Mallory joined them for lunch. She was sweet and kind—studiously avoiding any reference to her daughter's birthday dinner—but

Ann could not bring herself to offer more than the briefest possible polite replies to any questions directed at her. She was too aware of Matthew Fielding watching her, listening. The moment the meal was over she gave the excuse of having to pack, and left mother and son together.

She felt hopelessly agitated, almost desperate to get away from Fernlea and close herself into her own home. She would be all right tomorrow, she kept telling herself. The terrible tension she felt with Matthew Fielding would pass once they were back in the impersonal environment of the office.

Her suitcase was ready to go within ten minutes. Ann made sure she was leaving the room as tidy as when she had first entered it. When there was nothing more to do she carried her suitcase down to the foyer, left it at the foot of the staircase, then returned to the patio where mother and son were still seated.

'I'm ready to go when you are, sir,' Ann said. 'Where would you like me to wait for you?'

'Carmody——' he growled.

'Sit down here with me, Ann,' his mother hurriedly invited. 'Matt can come and collect you when he's ready. Go on, dear,' she urged her son. 'You know how you hate Sunday afternoon traffic back to the city. Better to get an early start.'

He threw a suspicious look at his mother's bright-eyed expression. 'You harangue me to come home, then you can't wait to get rid of me. At least be consistent, Mother,' he said drily.

'I am, Matt. You just don't appreciate how consistent I am.'

He rolled his eyes and stood up. 'Save me from women,' he muttered, and flicked Ann an irritated look as he passed her.

Having angled the opportunity to see Mrs Mallory alone, Ann relaxed on to the chair next to her. No way would she have spoken a word in front of Matthew Fielding, but she had nothing against his mother, and her own good manners insisted that she make some reply to Ellie's plea.

'Mrs Mallory, I think you must know that your daughter wrote me a note last night. Would you please let her know that I appreciated her sympathy, and have no hard feelings towards her. It was just...' she gave a rueful shrug '...one of those things.'

'I'm sorry too, Ann,' the older woman said softly. 'I'm glad we have this chance to talk together. I didn't like to intrude on your privacy, after last night. Of course, your life is your own business. We had no right...' She sighed, and offered an apologetic smile. 'I won't go on with that. I only want you to know that I would welcome your company again. Please don't feel awkward about coming to Fernlea if Matt wants you to.'

'Thank you. You're very kind,' Ann said stiffly, remembering the speculation that had been in the older woman's eyes when she had returned to the lounge last night. Surely to heaven she didn't think there was a chance of something more than a business relationship developing between her and Matthew Fielding?

'Matt was a very lonely boy,' his mother said sadly. 'His father died when he was very young, and we lived in the country with no close neighbours. He was eleven when I remarried, and, even though I had Ellie soon afterwards, it was then time for Matt to go away to boarding-school for his education. Such difficult years . . .'

She looked hopefully at Ann, who was feeling intensely embarrassed by the confidence. What Mrs Mallory was hoping could not possibly eventuate. It was madness to even entertain the thought! Ann didn't even like Matthew Fielding on a personal level. And he didn't like her, either! Nevertheless, it seemed rude to try and turn the conversation on to something else.

'And for all his success now,' Mrs Mallory continued, 'and all the business people he has around him, I know Matt is still lonely. I do wish he would stop long enough to get married and have a family. I'm sure he'd make a good husband and father, if he put his mind to it. He's been so kind to me, and helped Brian and Ellie with finance for their vet clinic——'

Ann instantly latched on to the words. 'A vet clinic? I didn't realise Brian was a veterinary surgeon,' she prompted.

Mrs Mallory obligingly took the lead, and talked happily about her son-in-law's wide practice in the local district.

To Ann's enormous relief, it wasn't long before Matthew Fielding appeared, attaché case in hand. His mother accompanied them out to the car and waved them off. No sooner were they through the gates than Matthew Fielding opened up in an accusatory voice.

'You were chatting very cosily to my mother.'

'I'm sorry, sir. If you prefer me to keep silent in future——'

He swore.

Ann shut her mouth tight and looked out of the side window.

They travelled a third of the way to Sydney in stony silence. The tension in the car could have been cut with a knife.

'My mother sees every woman I bring home, employee or otherwise, as a potential wife. If she was giving you her encouragement routine, forget it!'

Each word was a cold, virulent bite. Ann replied in like tone. 'Mr Fielding, what your mother sees is irrelevant. You would probably be the last man in the world I would ever see as a potential husband.'

'I am well aware of that, Carmody,' he snapped. 'I simply did not want you to think I had given my mother any grounds for her fond delusions. And I hope you made your position just as clear to her as you have to me!'

Ann reined in her temper, determined not to let him break her control. 'It was unnecessary,' she replied in a calm, flat voice. 'I do not believe in shattering other people's dreams. Sometimes it's all they have.'

He made no comment, and they travelled the rest of the way in an even stonier silence. Ann had the impression that his mind was working furiously, but he gave no clue as to what it was working on. His face was set in grim determination and his eyes remained fixed on the road.

If Matthew Fielding was lonely, Ann thought angrily, he undoubtedly deserved to be. He certainly had the knack of putting people off. Not that she wanted to be friendly with him—he could keep himself to himself for the rest of his life, for all she cared!

When they arrived at her apartment block in Wollstonecraft, he carried Ann's suitcase to her door and dropped it there. 'Happy dreams,' he said curtly, and strode off before she could thank him.

He was cold and curt all week leading up to the convention. He even seemed to evade looking directly at her. It was as if he was determined to ignore her existence as far as it was humanly possible, given their work situation.

All of which suited Ann admirably. She did the same thing. But, despite the cold war and the iron curtain she mentally constructed between them, nothing seemed to ease the tension she felt in his presence. She was aware of him continually. And she sensed that he was just as aware of her. Occasionally she caught herself remembering the strong virility of his body. He stamped that image on her mind all the more strongly when he floored her with another shopping demand.

It was Friday, their last day in the office before flying up to Queensland for the convention. Ann delivered a pile of correspondence for his signature before taking her lunch-break. For once he lifted his head, and there was a grim battle-light in his eyes as he spoke.

'While you're out, Carmody, buy me six pairs of underpants. Holeproof Daks. Ninety centimetres. Do I need to spell out more to you?'

Ann returned his gaze with barely contained fury. 'That's up to you, sir.'

'It had better not be, Carmody,' he threatened.

A weird feeling assailed her heart. He looked as if he hated her. Ann bit her tongue. If he wanted to fire her over six pairs of underpants, then he could do it, she thought wildly, and she would give him every reason to.

He probably didn't need underpants at all. More than likely, he was deliberately using this humiliating ploy to emphatically assert his authority over her—or some other darker form of domination that his ego required. But she would see him in hell before she would ever knuckle under it!

Six pairs!

It gave her a certain pleasure—a heady sense of freedom—to be utterly outrageous. It made her wonder if that was how her mother had felt when she had deliberately shocked people.

The salesman who served her was grinning from ear to ear by the time she had made her full selection. She had collected a white pair printed with red hearts, a red pair with fawn hands running all around it, a black pair with yellow noughts and crosses, a blue pair with white stars, that was really quite conservative, a green pair featuring black arrows, and a tan pair with white snowflakes.

She asked the sales assistant to parcel them up in brown paper with lots of sticky-tape so that no one could peek at the contents. If Matthew Fielding wanted to check her purchase, he would have to tear open the parcel.

She returned to the office in a mood of reckless defiance, but she did not let it show. She was completely poker-faced as she placed the parcel on his desk. 'Your underpants, sir,' she said coolly.

He stared at the parcel, then slowly lifted his gaze to hers. He probed her eyes for a long, nerve-stretching moment, avid for some sign that he had got to her in some way. Although it took every ounce of will-power she had, Ann kept her expression absolutely neutral.

'I trust they will be satisfactory?' he bit out.

'I'm sure they will wear well, sir,' Ann said confidently.

The parcel remained on his desk, unopened, all afternoon. If it was a ploy to unnerve Ann, it certainly worked. She swung between an urge to race out and buy plain underpants in order to effect a swap, and a stubborn determination to stick to her guns. When she left for the day the parcel was still there—a ticking bomb. The only question was...when would it explode?

Ann dithered all day Saturday. She shouldn't have done it. She really shouldn't. But the shops were open. If it hadn't been some contest of will— sheer malevolence on his part—if he really needed them, Matthew Fielding could go out and buy as many plain underpants as he liked. He didn't have to wear the ones she had bought.

Besides, he had a low opinion of her morals, anyway. With the selection she had made, she was only confirming what he already thought. And serve him right for asking her to do it.

Underpants!

That really was the bottom line!

By Sunday morning Ann's bravado was feverishly high. She packed her clothes for the convention, dressed in the now customary grey suit, called a taxi, and proceeded to Mascot Airport, where she had arranged to meet her boss in the Captain's Club lounge.

He was there.

And he didn't say a thing about underpants.

He read the *Bulletin* magazine while they waited for their flight to be called. Ann read *Time* magazine. Her eyes didn't focus very well, even though she wore her glasses. Matthew Fielding didn't seem to be turning too many pages, either.

It was a relief when the awaited announcement came. They boarded the plane together and settled side by side in their first-class seats. The stewardess offered drinks. Ann took an orange juice. Matthew Fielding took champagne. The take-off was smooth, and Ann's nerves gradually settled to a more acceptable level of tension. She had decided that Matthew Fielding had inadvertently left his parcel of underpants in the office, still unopened.

'Feeling good, Carmody?' he asked, startling her with the question.

'Fine, thank you,' she replied, darting a wary glance at him.

His eyes locked on to hers, dark and dangerously intense. 'Enjoy it while you can,' he said silkily. 'Because if anyone at this convention should catch me with my trousers down, Carmody, I shall take great pleasure in killing you.'

She suddenly had a full-blown image of him wearing the hearts, or the snowflakes, or the hands, and she had to work desperately hard to quell a hysterical desire to laugh. Which would be suicidal.

Since his need had apparently been genuine, she had no option left but to be completely honest and state her feelings on the matter. She schooled her voice to carry the conviction in her heart without being too emotional about it.

'One of the reasons I did not follow a singing career, Mr Fielding, was that I don't care to be exploited by other people, as I saw my mother exploited. Nor will I be exploited by you because I am a woman. I have a certain level of qualifications which you demean when you demand that I do your shopping simply because I am a woman.'

Ann's eyes glittered her challenge at him as she added, 'If you were me, sir, how would you feel about that?'

The hardness in his eyes wavered. He frowned and looked away. It was a long time before he answered, and he did not speak directly to her.

'If I had not heard you sing, Carmody, I would waive your argument without a second thought. To my mind, you should do what I ask—what I pay you for—to the best of your ability. But...since you feel so strongly about it...you do enough...without shopping,' he conceded grudgingly.

An indefinable load lifted off Ann's heart. 'I am sorry about the underpants, sir,' she said impulsively. 'It was the end of a hard week. I went overboard.'

'Yes, you did go overboard!' he snapped. Then unaccountably he heaved a deep sigh and threw her a rueful smile. 'But you're right. It was a hard week.'

Their eyes caught and held. It was barely for a second, but she saw a flash of raw vulnerability that found an instant echo inside herself. He grimaced and shook his head as he averted his gaze.

'I hope to heaven this next week is easier,' he growled.

CHAPTER SEVEN

SHE had won her point, or at least won the concession her pride demanded from him. Ann knew she should be feeling a flood of triumph, or, at the very minimum, a sweet wave of satisfaction. Instead, she was plunged into turmoil again.

Over the years she had found many men pleasantly attractive, but none had ever drawn the strong sense of empathy that Matthew Fielding sometimes evoked. And she didn't even like him! She liked even less the threat he posed to her control, to her sense of stability.

Why him? she thought angrily.

It had to stop!

Particularly when they were going to be in such close proximity for the next seven days. She simply had to get herself on an even keel and stay there. Except, with Matthew Fielding, nothing ever turned out that simple. It was very disturbing.

A white stretch Cadillac was waiting for them at Brisbane Airport. Ann appreciated the extra room in the luxury limousine. Although she had sat closer to Matthew Fielding on the flight up, riding with him in a car somehow heightened her awareness of his powerful masculinity. And it was a forty-five-minute trip to the Gold Coast.

She kept her eyes averted from him as much as possible. Just glancing at his trousered legs was enough to push unwanted thoughts across her mind. The car turned on to the freeway, and Ann felt rather than saw Matthew Fielding turn his gaze on to her.

'I hope you don't have some female liberationist objection to acting hostess at the drinks hour in my suite this evening.' His voice held an aggressive tone that warned Ann he had conceded as much as his own pride allowed. 'I prefer not to have a hotel waiter in on private talks with my executives,' he added with pointed purpose.

'No objection at all, sir. That's business,' Ann said decisively. She was actually looking forward to meeting his top men, wondering if she could ever match them, let alone beat them.

'Fine! One of these days I'll get you to define your job for me, Carmody,' he said very drily. 'It might save me some nasty surprises.'

She gave him a flat stare. Her mind questioned whether Matthew Fielding would ever consider a woman for an executive job, no matter how capable she was. 'I hope, sir, I've given you some pleasant surprises, too,' Ann said stiffly.

'You have,' he acknowledged. 'Which is why you're still with me. Despite the aggravations. Now, tonight, I want you to do a summation for me, Carmody. I want your impressions of my top men.'

Surprise rippled through Ann, but she didn't let it show. He had to respect her opinion to have said that. And she certainly respected his, when it came to business. 'I'm sure you've chosen well, sir, or the company wouldn't be as successful as it is,' Ann commented with complete sincerity.

'Mmm ... they're working under relentless pressure. Some people thrive on autonomy. But it can also break them. I've allowed these men to develop their own structures within their area of responsibility—so long as they themselves remain accountable for the research on new acquisitions and developments. No passing the buck to those lower down the ladder. Question is, can they keep developing?' He frowned. 'It's tough on marriages if the wives aren't pulling with them. You can check that out as well, Carmody.'

She looked at him in horrified distaste. 'You want me to ask them personal questions about their lives? Like a spy?'

His grimace instantly discounted that idea. 'Of course not. But I do get better work from people who are happy. I pay them a lot, and I reward effort with equity in the company, so I keep ensuring they're satisfied with their place in my organisation. I don't want anything to do with their private lives, but if I can fix a problem, I will. I'm footing the bill for their wives to have a holiday at the Mirage while the convention is on. We'll all dine together tonight.' His eyes glittered at her. 'You're different, and I'm sure you'll find it difficult to believe, but the fact is, I can't afford to get close to those women. You wouldn't credit the offers I get,' he said in a tone of bitter disgust, 'even from supposedly happy wives. And I can tell you, Carmody, my men are more important to me than any woman testing out her desirability with the boss.'

She wasn't so different, Ann thought wretchedly, remembering her deliberation over the cheongsam. And for the first time she comprehended the truth of Matthew Fielding's situation. He didn't think he was irresistible. He was simply sick to death of women throwing themselves at him. His strong sex appeal, combined with his wealth and power, inevitably made him a compelling target, and, if she really set her prejudice aside, Ann couldn't blame him for taking some of the offers. He wouldn't be human if he didn't.

In some ways, she supposed, it was the same as it had been for her mother. So many hangers-on to fame and beauty. Temptations...the hope that this time it might be different, better, lasting. Needs that were never quite answered.

'I can see it must be difficult for you,' she acknowledged sympathetically.

'Difficult!' he mocked, then, in a tone of heavy irony, 'You don't know the half of it. But to resume my point, you're a woman, Carmody. Surely you can see if those wives are happy and not putting on a false front? Or is that too much to ask?'

'What will you do if they're not happy?' Ann asked, cautiously reserving judgement until he answered.

He shrugged. 'I like to be aware of potential problems. Schedules can sometimes be juggled. Time off. A trip overseas. Something to relieve the strain.' He gave her a sardonic smile. 'Does that meet with your approval?'

His consideration for his men's welfare surprised and pleased her. It even made her like him...a little. 'I'll do what I can,' she promised, and before she could catch back the question it slipped off her tongue, 'Is that why you've never married? Because of——'

Appalled at her gaffe, she clamped her mouth shut and turned her head away. 'Please strike that question, Mr Fielding,' she said stiffly. 'It's none of my business.'

He gave a soft little laugh. 'Don't worry, Carmody. A little normal curiosity won't dirty your pristine record of reassuring me of your total disinterest. In actual fact, I've considered marriage several times, if only to eliminate the irritating, time-consuming business of finding someone I like well enough to sleep with on some kind of satisfactory, regular basis. Not to mention having someone to organise my social life, see that my laundry is done on time...' he shot her a hard, mocking look as he added '...and do any shopping I require.'

The liking he had earned just a few moments earlier died a swift death. His comfort! His convenience! Ann contemptuously surmised that all he thought he had to bring to a marriage was his body and his wealth.

There might be some women who would settle for that, but not Ann. And she didn't believe that any woman who did would be happy with her bargain for very long. When it came right down to it, no matter how much money you had, you could only wear one set of clothes at a time, drive one car at a time, live in one place at a time. And all that time could become very dreary if there was nothing else in the relationship.

Except sex.

Mitzi had certainly sounded quite satisfied with that. But Mitzi wasn't married to him, either.

Ann couldn't help wondering how good a lover Matthew Fielding was. Apparently he could not be quite as selfish in taking his own pleasure as he was in other areas of his life, or Mitzi wouldn't have been so eager for a repeat performance.

On the other hand, maybe it was just his body that excited Mitzi. Maybe she was a very physical sort of person, and Matthew Fielding didn't have to do much at all to satisfy her, except be the man he was. As much as Ann tried to repress her own awareness of his attraction, she had to admit that it stirred some female chemistry inside her.

'The only problem is,' Matthew Fielding continued, 'however attractive I find a woman initially, she invariably begins to bore me after a while. And, whatever the advantages, the thought

of living with a woman who bores me for the rest
of my life is quite enough to put me off marriage.'

'There is always divorce, sir,' Ann put in
flippantly.

'And have half of what I've built up ripped off
me?' he retorted derisively. 'Only a fool would go
that road, and one thing I'm not, Carmody, is a
fool.'

'No, sir.'

Her agreement effectively ended the conversation. He fell into a dark, brooding silence. Ann
wondered if Mitzi was beginning to bore him.

The limousine sped along to Southport. It turned
on to the 'Spit' where the Mirage Hotel was lo-
cated. The long peninsula embraced both the Pacific
Ocean and the Southport Broadwater, where rows
and rows of beautiful yachts were lined up along
the marina.

A few minutes later they drove up the driveway
which led to the reception area of the hotel. This
was so stunningly beautiful that when Ann stepped
out of the car she couldn't stop herself from
gawking around in dazed wonderment at the fantastic architecture of the place and the materials
used to decorate it.

The Mirage was aptly named. It shimmered with
light. It was possible to look straight through the
massive, glass entrance doors and the glass-panelled
wall at the back of the huge foyer to the ocean
beyond. The floor seemed almost to undulate with
the highly glazed tiles which Ann had read were

made from crushed sea shells, and their subtle colouring was wonderfully highlighted by their intriguing wavy pattern.

A man rose from one of the cane lounges in the open-air reception area and came forward to greet them. He was clean-cut, with short blond hair mixed with a sprinkling of grey, was fawn-suited, and had sharp blue eyes and a face that glowed with eagerness. About the same age as Matthew Fielding, Ann thought, as the two men shook hands with apparent pleasure.

He was introduced as Larry Pearson. Ann knew that he headed the company's tourist interests. It interested her that he did not give her a quick dismissive glance, but eyed her with sharp curiosity. Whether she wasn't what he had expected, or whether her close connection to Matthew Fielding made him wary, Ann did not know. He kept his expression genial and welcoming, and any opinion he formed about her carefully reserved.

'I've double-checked all the arrangements here. We can look forward to a smoothly run convention,' he said to Matthew Fielding as they moved into the foyer.

'Fine, Larry. The others here yet?'

'Bob and Alex and Nick and Terry all checked in this morning. With their better halves, as you directed,' he said with a happy grin. 'They're all out by the pool waiting for you to join them for a relaxing afternoon. Our respective teams will still be arriving right up until breakfast tomorrow morning.'

Ann was distracted by a roaring sound of water. She looked around and realised the foyer did not stretch to the panelled glass wall. A coral-coloured marble banister separated the foyer from a waterfall which dropped to the floor below. Her wandering gaze caught the glorious ocean-blue carpet squares set between the cane loungers. Patterned into the carpet were drifts of beautiful sea shells: mauve, pink, lemon, cream. The whole concept of the place was utterly delightful.

The bell-boy who had collected their luggage on a gleaming brass trolley paused beside them. 'Shall I show you to your rooms now, sir, or——?'

'Yes. See you later, Larry,' Matthew Fielding said in friendly dismissal, and took Ann's arm to steer her after the bell-boy.

She managed to move away from him in the elevator, putting the bell-boy and the luggage-trolley between them. She wished he would give up his courtesy touching. She knew it meant nothing but, every time he moved close to her, her nerves seemed to jump.

They went down to the floor below. As they passed the waterfall Ann noticed that the pool beneath it was scattered with coins. She smiled at the Trevi Fountain tradition, already persuaded that she also would like to return here.

Outside, a lagoon had been built to weave through the lush tropical gardens and it lapped the wall of the main complex. The bell-boy led them on to a bridge—a wide wooden walkway which crossed the lagoon to the swimming-pool and the accommodation wings.

The hotel was deliberately designed as a low-rise structure. Smooth, gleaming columns stretched from ground to roof-level, giving the buildings an air of cool elegance that was both aesthetic and restful. It did not really look like a hotel at all— not in any traditional sense. The shimmering light effect was maintained outside as well as inside, the buildings having been painted in a colour that was not quite white or pink, but suggestive of both.

Matthew Fielding was shown to his suite first— a private bedroom, a sitting-room that also accom- modated appropriate furniture for work meetings, and a marble bathroom with a spa-bath! All the interior decoration was most impressive, but Ann was just as pleased with her room, which was not only larger than any other hotel room she had ever been in, but also offered more comforts.

Apparently all the rooms were decorated in a similar style—subtle tangerine-pink and blue the main colours, beautifully toned lamps, com- fortable cane armchairs, a personal bar, facilities for tea or coffee-making, a television, a writing- desk, a king-size bed, and a wall of glass doors with a magnificent view of the ocean.

There was only one problem. She had been shown into her room through interconnecting doors from Matthew Fielding's suite!

All the time the bell-boy was showing her the buttons for the lighting and the radio and all the other services the hotel provided, including a button for personal butler service, Ann was conscious of those doors. The bell-boy hadn't shut them. He didn't shut them. And, virtually the moment he left, Matthew Fielding appeared in that still-open doorway, calmly unbuttoning his shirt as he spoke.

'I'm going along to the pool. You might as well come with me. Meet the others.'

Ann swallowed hard and dragged her eyes up from the fingers undoing buttons, from the black curls being revealed on that broad tanned chest. She didn't want to watch him swim. She would end up staring at that splendidly proportioned body of his. She knew she wouldn't be able to help herself. And if he saw her...

'Is that an order, sir?' she croaked.

He shot an irritated glance at her. 'No, it's an invitation, Carmody,' he said with an edge of sarcasm. The glance turned into a glare. 'Why is it that you turn everything I say into a challenge?'

'I'm sorry, sir. I don't mean to. I planned on unpacking and——'

'The butler will do that,' he snapped.

'I prefer to do it myself, sir.'

The glare seemed to get fiercer.

Before he could say any more, or do any more unbuttoning, Ann forced herself to take issue about the situation she found herself in.

'You didn't tell me our rooms would have interconnecting doors,' she blurted out accusingly.

'What did you expect?' he growled. 'For me to run down a corridor every time I had a thought I wanted to discuss with you, or get something noted down for future reference?'

His convenience again! 'I expected to have some privacy in between being at your beck and call, sir,' she grated. 'And not to have to see you undressing yourself in my doorway,' she added more forcefully.

The glare gathered a challenging glitter. 'Disturbs you, does it, Carmody?'

'I think it's over-familiar... yes, sir,' she said defiantly.

'Gives you ideas, does it, Carmody? Think I'm going to pop in and ravish you in the middle of the night?' he mocked.

'No!' she exploded.

'Good!' he snapped. 'Because let me tell you, Miss High and Mighty, I'm not so starved for sex that I have to stoop to that. And spare me the old-maidish prudery, because I know damned well where you come from, despite those bloody grey suits!'

Ann felt a burning wash of colour in her cheeks. She frantically regathered her dignity. 'I have a right to my own privacy, Mr Fielding. I want those doors kept closed, and I expect the courtesy of a knock if you want to speak to me. And I also expect you to wait until I open my door, if it has to be opened.'

His face hardened and his eyes seared her with venom. 'If you're also expecting to indulge yourself in a few extra-curricular activities while you're up here, Carmody, forget it! This week is all work. So when I knock, don't keep me waiting too long!'

He walked back into his suite and slammed the door after him. Ann hurriedly closed and locked the door on her side. Her legs were so shaky that she felt like crumpling on to the floor and bursting into tears. Which was stupid and weak and not like her at all, but Matthew Fielding got to her in a way no other man ever had. It was becoming harder and harder to cope with him.

She made it over to the bed and sat on it for some time, staring out at the ocean view, but not really seeing it. The butler called, but she declined his services. She unpacked in a desultory fashion, set up the cassette-player she had brought with her, and put in a tape. The music eventually succeeded in soothing her nerves, but she felt dull and listless and thoroughly miserable.

Matthew Fielding didn't know where she came from at all. He only knew about her mother. And that only in the most superficial and prurient way. Ann could count her own sexual experiences on two little fingers. The first had been when she was a student at Killara College—a once-only occurrence that had made her seriously consider that the act was highly overrated, and people could only be fooling themselves into believing it to be anything special.

The second time, several years later, she had allowed herself to succumb to a seductive siege that had promised much, but the final delivery had still been disappointing. She didn't know exactly what she had wanted—whether it had been her fault, or she hadn't been deeply enough involved in the relationship. Whatever the cause, Ann shied away when any man started pressing her for more than she was prepared to give.

She had an awful inner certainty that it would be different with Matthew Fielding—that he could arouse the excitement and passion that had eluded her before. She didn't understand it—didn't understand herself. Reason insisted that any kind of personal relationship with him would be the worst kind of folly. She didn't want it. And he certainly didn't! He had made that plain enough.

Afternoon drifted into early evening while Ann's mind revolved around her dilemma. The knock on her door came before she had resolved anything— certainly before she was ready to face Matthew Fielding again. She glanced at her watch. It was barely twenty minutes before she had to act hostess for him. He probably wanted to brief her on who liked what to drink. He definitely wouldn't appreciate being kept waiting.

She quickly unlocked her door and swung it open.

He had retreated into his sitting-room, his back turned to her as he spoke. 'Carmody, we need to get things straightened out,' he said, in a tight voice that was sharply edged with strain. He half turned and waved her in. 'Come and sit down. We have a few minutes before room service arrives to set things up.'

Ann closed her door and walked to one of the chairs around the table, feeling she couldn't take the more open exposure of an armchair. She sat down with as calm a composure as she could manage, and folded her hands in her lap. He took the chair on the opposite side of the table and regarded her with a hard, belligerent expression.

'I like the way you work, Carmody,' he stated. 'You're quick. You're smart. You pick things up that a hell of a lot of people would miss. You could be very valuable to me.' He paused and his lips thinned. 'But I am not going to be hassled by you for every damned thing I do and say.'

He banged his hands on the table, then curled them into white-knuckled fists. 'I was out of line with what I said to you before.' He shot an accusing finger at her. 'But you provoked me. I don't know if you did it deliberately or not, but it's got to stop, and it's going to stop right now.'

He tucked his finger back and banged his fist on the table. His eyes bored into hers with unrelenting purpose. 'We are here for this convention, and nothing... *nothing* is to interfere with our getting maximum input and output from this week. If that means you have to put up with a few things that offend your delicate sensibilities, then hold your tongue and put up with them. Do I make myself clear, Carmody?'

'Yes, sir,' she murmured, realising that he was probably right. She could see no other viable way of keeping the friction between them to a bare minimum. Besides, she had already won the really important points.

Far from appeasing him, her acquiescence seemed to raise his barely controlled ire. His finger flew out again, stabbing at her. 'And that's another thing! You "sir" me once more, Carmody, and I won't answer for the consequences. I am not your father! I'm not even old enough to be your father! And I sure as hell don't feel like your father!'

The fierce look he gave her was loaded with intense frustration. It sent prickles down Ann's spine. Did he feel the same discomfiting chemistry as she did? Did he want her...and not want her? Ann had to work some moisture into her mouth before she could reply.

'I'll do my best, Mr Fielding. And I do appreciate your remarks about my work. I would like...' She stopped, suddenly realising that the words she had been about to say had a far deeper truth than she wanted to recognise.

'Come on! Say it,' he commanded impatiently. 'I'm not totally unreasonable. What would you like, Carmody?'

She shook her head, appalled by the extent of her attachment to him. In so short a time! In the most adverse circumstances! 'It doesn't matter,' she said flatly.

'Oh, for heaven's sake! Don't play games with me. Spit it out.'

She met his angry eyes, searching for some spark of response in him. 'I would like to be valuable to you. That's all,' she said quietly.

He stared back at her, his anger diffused by an odd, harried look. 'Then do as I ask. That's all I want,' he insisted vehemently. 'Just do as I ask!'

Ann nodded resignedly. He remained typical—me Tarzan, you Jane. She couldn't expect him to ever change. He didn't want to muddy his nest, and he didn't want her pecking at it. She had to either accept that situation or resign, and she wasn't ready to resign . . . yet!

'As you wish, Mr Fielding,' she said submissively, but she knew in her heart that the kind of total submission this man would demand was impossible for her to give for any length of time.

It was so painfully ironic that it had to be this man Ann wanted . . . above all others.

CHAPTER EIGHT

MATTHEW FIELDING looked at Ann with deep-seated suspicion. It was clear that he no more believed in the totality of her submission than she did. The decision to test it was written on his face even before he spoke.

'I'd like you to call me Matt.'

The request—and his eyes gleamed with satisfaction in giving it—instantly flustered Ann. To be placed on first-name familiarity would inevitably draw her closer to him, and that would be highly dangerous to any peace of mind.

'I don't think it's appropriate for me——'

'I'll be the judge of that, Carmody.'

'But——'

'Can't you ever say anything without arguing?'

She bit her lip.

He noted the revealing action with even more satisfaction, and was positively good-humoured as he explained his reasoning.

'The men you are about to meet all call me Matt. Their wives call me Matt. I want them to know where you stand with me. And you stand high, Carmody. You're in tune with the way I do things. A second pair of ears and eyes. In one way you're closer to me than any of them. It's as well that they know that. It saves any misunderstandings in the future.'

As pleased as Ann felt with the status he was giving her, she did have one apprehension about his generosity. Her mouth curled with irony. 'You do realise it will probably give rise to a misunderstanding of another kind. Particularly since you saw fit to arrange adjoining rooms.'

He smiled. Like a shark. 'Should any of them have the temerity to think such a thing, Carmody, I have every faith in your ability to scotch the idea. And the wives will take one look at your grey suit, and that will be the end of that.'

He raised a mocking eyebrow. 'Am I wrong?'

It was a derisive admission that she had scored those points with him. She had to concede. 'No. Not this time. I'll call you Matt. And thank you for your confidence.'

He gave a harsh little laugh. 'You won't have any trouble fooling them. You're a very deceptive person, Angel Carmody. But don't worry,' he added as he saw her stiffen at the use of her full name. 'I have no intention of revealing that to anyone else. Let them find out for themselves, as I did. In the meantime, we shall work together, not against each other. Agreed?'

'Agreed.' She nodded warily. If he ever attempted to use her background as any kind of lever, she would make him regret it.

A knock on the door heralded the arrival of room service with a trolley. No sooner was everything set up than the executive team started arriving.

Boosted by Matthew Fielding's confidence in her, Ann did not take the backward seat she had first envisaged. She mixed, she questioned, she learnt, and savoured the dawning of respect she saw in each man's eyes. At one point she caught Matthew Fielding watching her with a look of secret amusement, and again experienced a flash of intimate communication. But it was only because she understood his way of doing business, she told herself.

The hour passed quickly. Ann did not have to manoeuvre a private conversation with anyone. Each man made it *his* business to seek a short tête-à-tête with her, and all their eyes were sharp and wary, even while their mouths smiled.

It was interesting to discuss her impressions with Matt afterwards, and there was no stress placed on their truce at all. Suddenly business was just business again, and the open sharing of ideas was exhilarating. They were agreed that Larry Pearson was the ultimate go-getter of the bunch, which was advantageous in his field of responsibility. The others were more reserved, but no less capable or shrewd; their drive and ambition was a long way from being diminished by continual pressure.

Matt assumed the role of escort when they walked up to the hotel foyer where the other couples had assembled. He introduced Ann to the wives before

they all adjourned to Horizons, the premier res-
taurant at the Mirage. Ann could not deny her
pleasure at being seated at Matt Fielding's right
hand, although she became aware throughout the
evening that he continually used her as a buffer to
distance himself from the other women.

Ann surreptitiously watched the wives. They all
seemed delighted to be here with their husbands,
enjoying the company and the beautiful food. And
certainly the faultless service and the ultra-elegant
setting did not go unappreciated. As far as Ann
could see, not one woman was discontented with
her lot. But a special night out was not the best
time to judge.

However, despite the little displays of affection,
and the obvious pride they showed in their husbands, there was not one woman who did not at
some time direct a glance of admiration at Matt
Fielding. It was as if he had a magnetism that they
could not deny, and Ann could not help wondering
whether any one of them would stay true to her
marriage if he beckoned.

It was a terribly cynical thought, but there was
a distinct air of competitiveness about these women
that told Ann they relished sharing the top of the
ladder with their spouses. Which was good—from
Matt's point of view. Their husbands' desire to
climb higher would always earn their full support.

But, of course, there could be no one higher than
Matthew Fielding in this company. And it wasn't
as if he only offered the power. Ann had to ac-

knowledge that no woman would ever be repelled by his looks. And his manner was perfectly charming to everyone all evening.

The meal came to an end. The after-dinner drinks and the conversation went on for a little while longer. Matthew Fielding tactfully reminded them all that a busy week lay ahead, and at this signal the party broke up.

As soon as they parted from the others and were on their way back to their rooms, Matt raised a questioning eyebrow at Ann. 'Well?' he prompted.

'You're right,' she admitted. 'Better for you to keep your distance. They admire you all the more for it. But I don't think you have to worry about work pressuring those marriages. Not one woman there would do anything but encourage her husband in his career. They're delighted with their positions.'

'No doubts?' Matt shot at her.

'Not in that sense, no. But no one can judge the more intimate side of a relationship from one meeting at a dinner-party,' she added drily.

He slid her a teasing look that set her pulse racing. 'You had them intrigued. Looking like a modern-day nun, drinking lemonade... which reminds me—what have you got against alcohol, Carmody?'

For some reason, she didn't mind telling him now. 'I've seen what it can do to people. It was a problem for my father. It usually is a problem for musicians... the places they work. The night-life. He died of liver damage when I was ten.'

He made no immediate comment. They walked on in a companionable silence. The evening had forged a sense of partnership that Ann hugged to herself with secret pleasure. She knew it couldn't last, but for the moment it was the closest she had felt to anyone apart from her mother.

'You've never touched drugs, either, have you, Carmody?' he suddenly said with quiet certainty.

'No, I haven't,' she answered just as quietly, wondering how much he understood about her. She tensed, half expecting him to ask about her sex-life, but he did not pursue that line.

He shook his head. 'You've had some kind of life, Carmody.'

She threw him an ironic smile as they reached the door which led from her room to the corridor. 'At least you couldn't call it boring.'

'No. And neither are you,' he murmured.

Ann's heart hammered in her chest. His soft remark had been like a caress on her soul, and she was deadly afraid of showing how deeply it affected her. She made a concentrated production of pushing the coded room-key into its slot and opening her door.

He said nothing more. He didn't move away. Ann's whole body vibrated with an electric awareness that he was waiting for some sign from her, yet she wasn't sure what he wanted. Perhaps he wasn't sure himself. The rules about their relationship had become blurred tonight.

'Goodnight,' she said quickly, barely glancing at him.

'Goodnight,' he returned gruffly, and walked on towards his door.

Ann made a slow ritual of washing and preparing for bed, doing her best to relax. But despite all her efforts she could not get to sleep. She felt overexcited and restless, and try as she might she couldn't get Matt Fielding out of her mind. Desperate for some calming distraction, she switched on the television and watched an in-house movie until her eyelids grew heavy.

She ended up using the same tactic every night as the convention wore on.

Matt did not invite her to go swimming with him again, although she knew he made use of the hotel pool every morning. Other company employees referred to their early morning swim with him. Ann wondered if they were really fitness fanatics, or simply courting approval. It was impossible to tell, but she noticed with some amusement that not one of the two hundred people at the convention looked out of shape.

The days were filled with high-power meetings and discussions, even over meals. Every morning there was breakfast by the pool with the top representatives of each division. Lunch was always spent in the catered conference-room. The evenings varied between formal dinners and buffet meals by the poolside. Throughout the whole week, Ann was the only constant at Matthew Fielding's side.

For the most part they lived and breathed business, and Ann enjoyed every minute of that. It was exciting and safe—all within her competence. And she enjoyed Matt's recognition of her competence. He liked talking to her about everything that was going on, and he insisted on her sharing a late supper with him in his suite each night.

However, he invariably ended up sliding a couple of personal questions at her that instantly changed the easy atmosphere. He did it offhandedly, as if her answers were only of mild curiosity to him— questions about her life at school, with her mother, other jobs she had held, her interest in music—but the watchfulness in his eyes, the quality of stillness about him as he waited for her reply, created a tension in Ann that immediately made her feel defensive.

'Why do you want to know?' she demanded one night.

He shrugged. 'Is there any harm in my knowing?'

The challenge was subtle, yet Ann felt a relentless purpose behind it. 'What do you want to win, Matt?' she fired at him point-blank.

His mouth twisted. 'Perhaps some peace of mind. You're a puzzle, Carmody, and I probably won't feel content until I work you out.'

'Then you'll find me boring,' she tossed at him, and said a very firm goodnight as she headed for the interconnecting doors.

But she was trembling when she locked the door on her side. She rested her forehead against it for a moment, and took a deep breath before turning into her room.

It was because she was different, because she didn't fall all over him, Ann argued to herself. If she ever weakened, ever gave him everything he wanted, that would be the end of it. She would inevitably lose the best job she had ever had, and she didn't want to lose it.

She switched on the television. The in-house movie was *Fatal Attraction*. Very apt, Ann thought, and watched it with semi-glazed eyes.

The convention ended and Matt held another private dinner for his executives and their wives as a celebratory gesture. Everyone agreed that the week had been an exciting success. Ann noticed that Matt drank more wine than usual, but he exhibited no signs of intoxication.

They sat around the table drinking coffee and brandy or port long after the meal had been cleared away. It seemed that no one wanted to make a move to end the evening. Ann was forced to visit the powder-room. Larry Pearson's wife, Amanda, also rose from the table, giving her a women-together smile and saying she would accompany her.

Which meant that Ann ended up having to wait while Amanda fiddled with her shoulder-length black hair and applied fresh make-up to her vivacious face. The bright hazel eyes kept darting curious looks at Ann in the mirror, and finally the curiosity slid into speech.

'Larry says you're terribly sharp and efficient. I guess you'd have to be...working for Matt.'

'He doesn't suffer fools gladly,' Ann replied with a dry smile. The way Amanda said 'Matt' gave him a godlike status.

'No. He's amazing, isn't he? Being with him all the time...don't you feel madly attracted to him?'

'He has his faults,' Ann said even more drily.

Amanda gave a little laugh. 'I suppose all men do, close up.' She slid a sly but intensely avid look at Ann. 'I've heard he's a marvellous lover.'

'I really wouldn't know,' Ann drawled, projecting total uninterest.

'Oh!' It was the sound of disappointment. 'Then you're not sleeping with him?'

Ann's shock was not altogether feigned. 'Whatever made you think that?'

'Please don't be offended. I certainly wouldn't think it a crime to sleep with Matt Fielding. But I didn't really think you were.' Her eyes flickered down Ann's grey suit and up again. 'It was just something Larry said.'

'Like what?' Ann demanded coldly.

Amanda sighed. 'I've put my foot in it, haven't I? When will I learn to keep my big mouth shut?'

'I would like to know what Larry said, if you don't mind.'

'Oh, nothing much,' was the airy reply.

'Word for word,' Ann insisted icily. She was not about to let the matter drop. If there was any gossip being spread about her and Matt Fielding, she wanted to scotch it right now. It was hard enough keeping her distance. It was totally unfair that she be branded as Matt Fielding's mistress when she wasn't.

Amanda shrugged. 'Well, if you'll forgive the rough vernacular, he said that you and Matt were as close as two peas in a pod. Inseparable. Everyone wondered.'

Ann's inner tension eased. She could well imagine Larry Pearson saying that. It was nothing.

'Then, of course, there's the way Matt looks at you . . . when you're not looking,' Amanda added slyly.

A little shiver ran down Ann's spine. 'Obviously, I don't know what you're talking about,' she said coolly.

The woman's smile was all too knowing. 'Well, I'd say tonight's the night. Lucky you.' She dropped her lipstick into her handbag, snapped the bag shut, and headed for the door.

'What do you mean by that?' Ann demanded, her heart fluttering in apprehension.

'Why, nothing,' Amanda retorted blithely, and pulled the door open as she added, 'It can't be anything if you're not agreeable. On the other hand, it's always a woman's privilege to change her mind. Are you coming?'

Ann returned to the table in terrible confusion of mind. Was Amanda Pearson simply being bitchy because Matt hadn't paid her as much attention as she would have liked? Or did she know something Ann didn't know?

How did Matt look at her when she wasn't looking?

Why was he drinking more than usual tonight?

Surely it was only a celebration thing . . . relaxing at the end of a long, work-packed week that had been very rewarding in terms of company business?

Perhaps Amanda was even envious of Ann's position at Matt's side. In any event, Ann was not about to give her any satisfaction from those snide remarks in the powder-room. She kept her gaze averted from Matt, and didn't once glance to see how he was looking at her. If he looked at her at all!

To Ann's intense relief, the party broke up shortly after her return to the table. Matt was uncharacteristically silent as they walked back to their accommodation wing. The evening and the company did not seem to have relaxed him. His whole body emanated tension. Even his voice sounded strained when he finally spoke.

'Come into my suite,' he invited. 'There's something I want to give you.'

They had reached Ann's door and she hesitated, recalling Amanda's words too vividly to feel comfortable about entering Matt's suite tonight. 'I thought we'd wound all the business up for this week,' she said, even as she chided herself for letting the woman's suggestive words affect her. Matt himself had given her no reason to be wary.

'It won't take long,' he assured her, firmly ushering her into his sitting-room.

He left her there and went into the bedroom. Ann did not make anything of it. She simply waited resignedly. She was tired and a little depressed that the week was over. Despite the tensions she had suffered, she had felt more brilliantly alive in Matt's company this week than she had ever done in her life.

He came back with a round velvet box which he handed to her. 'In appreciation of a job well done,' he said warmly.

Ann frowned at the unexpected gesture, not at all sure that she should accept a gift of jewellery from him. She opened the box with a tense feeling of apprehension, and stared disbelievingly at a double-stranded pearl choker with what looked like a diamond and sapphire fastening. If it was the genuine article—and Ann had no real doubt that it was—it had to be worth thousands and thousands of dollars.

She lifted dazed eyes. 'Matt, I can't take this from you.'

He frowned. 'I've just given it to you. I want you to have it. So don't give me any argument, Carmody.'

Ann shook her head. 'It's beautiful...but it's too much.'

'Nonsense!' he snapped. 'I gave all the other wives presents for putting up with us this week. Not personally, of course. I organised Larry to do that.

But I ordered this especially for you. Got the jeweller to deliver it to me today. And I'm not sending it back. In fact I'm going to put it on you right now.'

Ann stared in stunned realisation as he slowly lifted the pearls out of their box. Larry... Amanda...they must have known about this gift. And put the obvious interpretation on it. But were they right? What did Matt mean by it? What kind of gifts had the wives been given? As expensive as this?

Matt already had the necklace unfastened before Ann could find voice to protest. 'Matt, I'm not a wife,' she argued frantically. 'I've simply done the job you pay me for.'

He ignored her argument.

'No...please...no!' she cried, backing away from him as he stepped closer to put the pearl choker around her neck.

'Yes,' he rasped, his face darkening with determination.

Ann could see there was no fighting him over this. She stood stock still and allowed him to fasten the necklace around her throat, silently praying this was all there was to it. She didn't know what she would do if Matt tried to take some advantage of the situation. She didn't want him to.

Her skin leapt with prickling warmth at his touch. Her breath was trapped somewhere in her tightened chest. She closed her eyes in a desperate attempt to shut him out. But then she was more aware of other things: the tangy scent of his aftershave lotion, the feathering caress of his fingertips as he straightened the pearls to his liking. It terrified her that he might feel the wildly leaping pulse in her throat, and she felt sick with the need to feel and know more of him.

'You can open your eyes, Carmody. The deed is done,' he said sardonically. 'I won't have to touch you again.'

Relief flooded through her. It was all right. Amanda was wrong. Her eyelashes fluttered up.

Matt hadn't stepped back. The tone of his voice had been deceptive. His face was so close to hers, she couldn't mistake the dark hunger in his eyes— the need to take and dominate and possess all of her. He had looked at her like that once before...at Fernlea. And at dinner tonight? Was this what Amanda Pearson had seen?

Ann panicked. Her mind shot out a babble of words as she side-stepped away from him on appallingly shaky legs. 'Thank you. You're very kind. Please excuse me now—there's an in-house movie I want to watch. *Dancing in the Moonlight*. It's got Robert Golding in it. He's the most sensual man I've ever seen on screen.'

A flush of furious frustration suffused Matt's face. 'Carmody, for heaven's sake!' His hand reached out for her.

She backed towards the interconnecting doors, unable to tear her eyes away from the turbulent desire in his. 'I can't miss it. The dancing is terrific.

I've never seen better of its kind,' she rattled on, barely knowing what she was saying.

Then she bumped into the door, and somehow she managed to turn and wrench it open. But, even when it was closed behind her and Matt Fielding safely shut away on the other side of it, Ann could still see that dark wanting in his eyes. And it wasn't going to go away. No matter what she said or did, it wasn't going to go away. Somehow they had come too far together this week. And there was no going back to a rational relationship.

Had it ever been rational? Ann wondered miserably.

Hadn't they been reacting against each other from day one?

All the stupid things she'd said and done—the nonsense about younger men, the grey suits, the frilly dress-shirt, those provocative underpants— extreme reactions! But he wasn't blameless, either...goading her at every opportunity. Even so, if she had just been normal and natural—even reasonable—they might not have come to this.

Disgusted with herself, Ann stripped off the unattractive grey suit and the white tailored shirt. She kicked off the dowdy black mini-heels and removed her stockings. The only garment she left on was the pink silk and lace teddy she wore next to her skin. That at least reflected her true self.

She moved over to the vanity-mirror so she could see how to unfasten the pearl choker. Accepting the necklace had been madness. It had to be returned.

And as quickly as possible. Before Matthew Fielding got any more ideas. Tomorrow. First thing tomorrow.

Her fingers slid over the richly gleaming pearls as she removed them from her throat. Why had he bought them for her? Had he planned the gift as a bribe to get her into his bed? He had shown himself cynical enough to believe that would work on any woman.

And the only reason he wanted her was because she wouldn't give in to him! She had recklessly challenged his sexuality, his ego, his authority, almost everything that he was; the only way he could answer that challenge was to get her to surrender to him. That was all it was for him. Winning!

A terrible emptiness tore through her stomach. It was so painfully ironic…the one man she wanted above all others…and he would never believe it. She had to get away from him and stay away. It was the only sensible thing to do.

Tears welled into her eyes. She took off her glasses and dashed the moisture away. Sick at heart and weary of mind, she wandered listlessly over to the glass doors and slid one open. The sound of the ocean rolled into her ears. It was a dark night. No moon. No stars. It suited her mood. She leaned against the door-frame and didn't care about the tears that trickled down her cheeks.

How long she stood there, Ann didn't know. Time was immaterial. The sharp rat-a-tat on the door from Matthew Fielding's suite startled her out of her dark reverie. Her heart leapt in agitation. Why would he knock at this hour? What did he want?

She wouldn't answer it. Whatever he had to say to her could wait until morning. She couldn't bear to see him again tonight. She turned her face back to the night outside, determined to ignore any further knock as well.

The metallic click of the door being opened sent a frisson of fear through her whole body. He wouldn't dare...would he? She jerked around as Matthew Fielding came striding into her room, then froze into stunned immobility when she saw how he was dressed.

He came to an abrupt halt the moment his gaze found her, and his air of barely suppressed violence vanished in an instant, the wild expression on his face totally transformed to something else...something that held Ann transfixed.

CHAPTER NINE

MATT looked at her as though she were a vision he couldn't quite believe, his eyes grazing over the brief concoction of silk and lace that did little to hide the femininity of her body, and much to enhance it. The pale, bare shapeliness of her legs, the soft roundness of her arms and shoulders, the long, graceful neck ... his fascinated gaze fed on all of them in nerve-quivering slow motion before drifting up to her mouth, and finally to her tear-glazed blue eyes.

He wore a short dark red bathrobe which revealed a deep V of his naked chest. His legs were bare. Ann wondered if he had anything on underneath his bathrobe, and she felt light-headed at the thought of his virile nakedness. She swallowed hard. Her mind was a chaotic mess. All her defensive instincts came screaming to the fore.

'You had no right to come into my room!' she said in harsh accusation.

His expression snapped back to glowering belligerence. 'I knocked! You didn't answer.'

'At this time of night?' she screeched.

'You're still up, aren't you?' he hurled back at her.

'That's not the point!'

'Oh, yes it is! It's precisely the point! I don't be-lieve everything I'm told. Not even by you. So I thought I'd make a little check,' he said with biting sarcasm. His eyes snapped black fury at her as he added, 'And you are not watching that damned movie with that...that smarmy gigolo in it! So what's going on, Carmody?'

'What business is it of yours?' Ann challenged fiercely. 'And in the interests of accuracy, Robert Golding wasn't a gigolo in it, anyway. He was a——'

'You lied!' Matt thundered at her.

'I changed my mind,' she retorted defiantly.

'Oh, sure!' he said, with heavily loaded derision. His eyes glittered over her and his arms lifted and swept out in a mocking presentation gesture. 'And that's what you wear under your sexless grey suits. I'm glad I found out about that, too. It dem-onstrates my point even more clearly. You are de-liberately...deliberately   deceptive,   Angel Carmody!'

Ann's chin automatically lifted in disdain of any criticism. 'I wear what I like where no one can see.'

His hands came to rest on his hips. 'All part of the pattern, isn't it?' he simmered at her. 'The pattern of deceit. But let me tell you, Angel Carmody, it won't work any more.'

The mocking way he used her full name again stiffened Ann's backbone. With as much dignity as she could muster, she said, 'If that's your message, Mr Fielding, consider it delivered. Now, please, get out!' Then she deliberately turned her head away and stared back out at the ocean.

'Damn you!'

The words exploded from him with vehement passion, and in the same instant he exploded into action, striding across the room, hauling her away from the view, taking a bruising grip on her upper arms and shaking her while more words spat from his contorted face.

'It's all lies, isn't it? The sex orgies with younger men, your expertise in the sound of satisfaction, lusting after a two-bit screen star. Why did you lie to me?'

The black violence in his eyes shook Ann more than the rough handling. 'Yes. They're lies,' she cried, no longer in control of anything. 'You wouldn't recognise the truth, anyway. You're so damned full of yourself, you only see what you want to see.'

'Then tell me!' he raged at her. 'Tell me the truth. And heaven help us both, because I can't take any more of this.'

'*You* can't take any more?' Ann was almost incoherent with her own fury and frustration. 'You get your hands off me! Get your damned eyes off me! Get away from me before I scream this whole hotel down!'

His fingers dug deeper into her flesh. His eyes blazed with a mad determination. 'I'll know what I want to know first,' he grated, and with ruthless strength he pinned her body to his with one arm and used his other hand as a vice-like clamp around her head. There was no tenderness in the mouth that took hers, only a relentless, devouring need to plunder it into submission.

Shock held Ann powerless for several completely lost moments: the shock of his bare thighs pressing against hers—hard, hair-roughened, aggressively masculine; the shock of his warm, firm flesh under her hands, which were helplessly trapped against his chest; the shock of his mouth invading hers and arousing a wild storm of sensation that sapped her mind of any self-determination.

The desire to respond clawed through her, but there was no caring for her in what he was doing. Possession...domination...that was all it was, and her heart shrivelled at the thought of giving in to it. No matter how much she wanted him, she would die rather than let him take her on this basis.

Her mouth felt bruised and debauched when he finally withdrew his assault. And her emotions were in shreds, torn so many ways that she could not face him with any dignity at all...righteous or otherwise. Tears burnt her eyelids and squeezed under her lashes.

'Please...' She could barely speak, and didn't care that she was begging. 'Please...let me go,' she managed in a hoarse whisper.

His hold on her gentled. 'Ann...I...' He made a harsh guttural sound. His hands slid away and he stepped back from her.

It left her feeling horribly exposed to him. The need to cover herself was so paramount, she broke into a staggering run towards the wardrobe at the other end of the room. Her legs were so shaky, it was difficult to direct them, and, half blinded by tears, she blundered against the edge of the bed and almost fell.

A hand grasped her arm.

She beat at it in panicky despair. 'No...No...'

'I was only trying...' The hand was removed.

She straightened herself, took several gulping breaths and pushed on to the wardrobe. Her hand found the poppy housecoat more by feel than sight, and she dragged it out and wrapped herself in it, tying the belt with savage tightness. She dashed the tears away from her eyes with the back of her hand and tried desperately hard to regain some composure.

'Ann...what can I say?' He sounded guilty, almost anguished. 'I didn't come in here to do that. You goaded me...I didn't mean to...it just...happened...'

His self-serving words burnt a righteous anger through Ann's limp body. She swung around to face him with his lie. Her voice shook with outrage at the indignities she had suffered. 'I didn't ask you in here, Matt Fielding! And don't you dare blame me for your rotten urges. As for it...just happening...it was very convenient for you to just happen into my room wearing only a bathrobe!'

His face went red. 'I didn't think . . . I didn't intend coming in here! I was going to bed . . . and I switched on that damned movie . . .' His eyes shot bitter accusation at her. 'There are some things a man just can't take. And you——'

'Oh, yes! It's always the woman's fault, isn't it?' she blasted at him. 'Only that excuse isn't going to work for you. There's one big flaw in your argument. I knew that tonight was the night. So it's no use your pretending otherwise.' Her eyes flashed her contempt. 'You meant it, all right. It just didn't work out the way you planned it, and that's what you couldn't take. The all-conquering Matt Fielding turned down for a picture on a little screen!'

All trace of guilty anguish had fled from his face. He glared back at her in furious resentment. 'You'd better explain yourself, lady!' he grated. 'Because I tell you right now that I had nothing planned. Nothing! I might be guilty of a momentary aberration, but I won't be accused of anything more than that.'

Ann eyed him with weary disgust. 'This is utterly pointless. I don't want to argue. I just want you to go. And take your pearls with you. They're right there on the dressing-table below the mirror. My resignation from the company is effective as of now. We have nothing more to say to each other.'

He folded his arms in aggressive determination. 'I'll go when we've cleared this up, and not before. What did you mean—you knew that tonight was the night? The night for what?'

'You think you can bluff your way out of it?' she mocked savagely, her inner pain adding its raw edge to her voice. 'I was fool enough not to believe her until you gave me the pearls. And then . . . then I tried to block what you had in mind, but you wouldn't give up, would you? You had to come in after me. You couldn't stand not winning!'

His face ran through a gamut of expressions . . . bewilderment, affront, an appalled understanding, and finally blistering anger. 'Who?' he barked grimly. 'Who is *her*, and what did she say to you?'

Ann's outburst had completely depleted her energy. She felt as if she had been dragged through a wringer. She waved a limp hand in dismissal. 'What does it matter? You proved her right.'

'Larry . . . Amanda . . .' His eyes narrowed as the connections flew through his mind. 'She went to the powder-room with you. You were gone a long time.' He smacked a fist against his palm and his eyes glared with furious contempt. 'That hot-eyed bitch had to have a shot at you, didn't she?'

He didn't wait for an answer. He stormed off to the other end of the room, pacing off his rage. 'Bitch! Bitch! Bitch! Just because I showed I preferred you to her. You in your drab grey suits. So she had to pull you down. Make you less than she was. I can just imagine how it went . . .'

He spun around, his face twisted in bitter mockery as he mimicked the conversation. ' "Has he laid you yet?" "Certainly not," you'd say.

"Well, obviously tonight's the night," she'd say with her snaky, suggestive smile. "He's got you all lined up with an expensive gift that will buy your favours quick enough."'

His eyes glittered his certainty at her. 'Right, Carmody?'

'Close enough,' she snapped, unsure where he was leading to, and feeling confused by the depth of his venom.

His mouth turned vicious. 'So I'm neatly entrapped, aren't I? No matter what my intentions, I'm condemned. Unquestioned. Unheard.'

He walked towards her, absolutely steaming, his words whipping out with laced acid. 'Well, let me tell you, Carmody, you underestimate my powers of perception. Which, where women are concerned, is considerably jaundiced. With good reason. But I have tried...I have tried very hard this week...not to step on your toes. To treat you how you want to be treated. Not to impose unduly on your time or privacy. To respect your wishes...even against my own.'

He came to a halt a couple of metres from her and dragged in a deep breath. His eyes seared hers with bitter challenge. 'Have you any complaint about the way I have conducted myself in your company this week...apart from tonight's madness?'

She could not honestly fault him. Since their heated confrontation on the day they had arrived at the Mirage, he had acted precisely as he outlined, and she could not blame him for her own tortured emotions. 'No. I enjoyed this week with you,' she answered grudgingly.

'Right!' he snapped. 'Now we come to tonight. Surprising as it may seem to you, I am well aware that your favours cannot be bought, Carmody. The way you spoke about your mother...the way you've stood up to me...it would take a bigger fool than I am to think you could be exploited in any way whatsoever. Grant me that much sense and sensibility.'

He paused, waiting for the concession from her. Ann felt even more confused. She could not discount the desire she had seen in his eyes—it had been too starkly real—but neither could she deny the logic of his argument.

'You...you have a reputation as a womaniser, Matt,' she said, fumbling through her thoughts. 'The way you speak about women...the little regard you hold them in. And I knew what you thought that night at Fernlea when you learnt about my mother.'

'You had given me reason to think what I did,' he reminded her tersely.

She nodded in miserable acknowledgement, too mortified by her own self-defeating conduct to defend herself.

'I gave you the opportunity to explain the next morning. I would have listened,' he said with deep frustration. 'But you made yourself so damned unreachable . . . frozen up tight. And I still don't understand why you lied about it in the first place.'

She felt too wretched to bother dissembling any more. 'You riled me that first day . . . lining us up as if we were nothing . . . picking me at random . . . then telling me I wasn't to fall in love with you. I was hitting back at you. It was stupid. You just made me so mad . . .'

'I know the feeling,' he said with pointed emphasis, and his eyes darkened with angry accusation. 'Why the hell do you have to react as though I'm a leper every time I touch you? It makes me want to——'

He bit down on the words and turned away, shaking his head as he paced back up the room. His shoulders rose and fell in a deep sigh. It did not seem to ease his frustrations. When he swung around, his face wore a beetling frown and he stabbed an accusing finger at her.

'You've got to admit, Carmody, you're a very provocative woman. I present you with a gift, which I've taken the time and trouble to choose myself . . .' his voice rose several decibels '. . . and all you can do is prattle on about your lust for some movie star!'

His finger dropped down. He drew his shoulders back. 'To say the very least, that wasn't courteous of you. No normal red-blooded man will take that kind of treatment lying down. I was wrong in . . . in going as far as I did. I lost my head . . . no doubt about it. It was a culmination of several provocations, of which I'm sure you're aware. Nevertheless, I was wrong, and I'm sorry I acted as I did. Can I say fairer than that?' he demanded tersely.

Ann didn't know what to think. Had she misread that look in his eyes? Was it only a reaction to the frustrations she had given him?

'Why did you buy me the necklace, Matt?' she blurted out, desperate for some excuse to stay with him, but not so masochistic as to invite her own self-destruction at his hands.

'Because I damn well wanted to!' he growled at her. He threw up his hands as if he'd been driven to the end of his tether. 'Can't I do what I want to? It was a whim—an extravagant whim, if you like—but I can afford extravagant whims!'

She stared at him, not accepting his explanation. Somehow it didn't ring true. He was protesting too much.

He saw she didn't believe him. He clenched his teeth in disgust and his eyes flashed fierce resentment at her. 'You like your pound of flesh too much, Carmody,' he grated.

'If you want me to disregard what happened tonight, Matt, you'd better tell me the truth,' she said flatly, giving no quarter over this.

She might . . . might be able to go on working for him if he didn't see her as a handy sexual commodity, but there were still her own feelings that had to be kept hidden.

He glowered at her. His answer came out in short angry bursts. 'Damn it! You made me feel guilty about some of the things I'd said and done. I wanted to please you. You said you wanted to be valuable to me. Well, you are. I thought I'd show you by giving you something you wouldn't buy yourself. The cost was nothing to me. It was simply a peace-making gesture. And if you can't accept that——'

He stopped, looking hopelessly harried as tears welled into her eyes.

Ann couldn't stop them. He had cared about her feelings. The relief...the pleasure...the regret that she had judged him so meanly... the tears just kept spilling out of a tidal wave of overwhelming emotions.

'Don't! Don't cry!' he appealed hoarsely. He charged towards her, then pulled himself to an abrupt halt, clenching his hands and looking even more harried. 'I mustn't touch her. Hell! What's a man supposed to do?' he muttered.

'I'm sorry,' Ann gulped. 'I'll... I'll be all right in a minute.'

He turned aside and picked up the pearls from the cupboard, turning the necklace roughly through his hands in a distracted fashion, waiting tensely for her to compose herself.

'I'm the one who should be apologising, not you,' he said gruffly. 'And I really am sorry that I've distressed you so deeply. Whatever the provocation, I had no right to... to molest you like that. I've never done such a thing before.'

Ann believed him this time. It had just happened...not planned at all. And, in all honesty, she had certainly given him some provocation. She wished he had kissed her differently...and that thought brought more tears.

He heaved a deep sigh and his voice rasped through an awkward plea. 'I don't want to lose you, Ann. I know it's asking a lot for you to overlook what I did, but I promise you it will never happen again.'

He stared gloomily at the pearl choker in his hands. 'I guess I'd better send this back. You won't want it now,' he said grimly.

'I do so want it,' she burst out, not stopping to think whether it was wise or not to accept such a gift from him, only knowing that she would treasure it, whatever else happened.

His gaze jerked back to hers in surprise.

Flustered and floundering, Ann tried to explain away her acceptance. 'It was very kind. I appreciate the thought behind it. I'm sorry I...but you must do what you wish, of course. Send it back, by all means. I don't deserve it after...after...'

'No. I want you to have it,' he insisted vehemently. He strode over and shoved the necklace into her hand. 'I bought it for you. It's yours. It looked good on you.'

'Thank you,' Ann whispered, her voice strangled by his nearness. She found herself staring at the black curls on his chest, and dragged her gaze up to his face.

He was staring at her, and the memory of the intimacy he had taken writhed between them.

He pulled an ironic grimace. 'And what the hell!' he said with forced lightness. 'Maybe I am too full of myself.'

'You're not, really,' Ann protested, then flushed at the eagerness of her denial. 'I mean...you wouldn't be where you are if you didn't have that kind of confidence in yourself. It...it stands to reason.'

He gave a dry laugh. 'Well, if it doesn't, Carmody, I'm sure you'll put me in my place. You have a definite gift for it.' He paused, and all humour fled as he quietly added, 'That is...if your resignation is now withdrawn.'

She couldn't quite meet his eyes. 'Yes. If that's all right with you.'

'That's settled, then,' he said quickly. 'I'm glad we've...um...come to a better understanding. Goodnight, Carmody.'

'Goodnight,' she echoed.

But he was already gone, as swiftly as he had come, the door clicking decisively shut behind him.

A long, quivering breath whispered from Ann's lips. The truth was hammering through her heart and mind—impossible to ignore or turn it into something else.

She loved him.

It wasn't simply that she found him more attractive than any other man she'd met. It wasn't just a case of wanting to know how it would be if he made love to her. And to pretend she enjoyed her job because it extended what abilities she had was another self-deception. Most of the pleasure was in being with him—sharing his thoughts, his ideas, his ambitions.

She had committed the unforgivable sin!

She had fallen in love with Matthew Fielding!

Deeply. Shatteringly. Irrevocably.

Ann felt a wrenching sympathy for the women who had preceded her as his personal assistant. How long had they managed to go on working for him before they had revealed their feelings . . . torn by the need for him to respond?

But he cared about her, Ann argued frantically to herself. She was valuable to him. He did not want to lose her.

Her fingers squeezed around the pearls he had given her. Surely she had to mean a great deal to him, since he had gone to so much trouble on her behalf . . . choosing and buying such an expensive gift . . . even if the money meant little to him? He certainly liked having her with him. And he found her physically attractive. There could be no doubt about that.

Maybe there was a chance—if she stayed with him—that he would fall in love with her. Maybe she would be different from all the others. There was hope . . . wasn't there? She did have reason to hope.

CHAPTER TEN

ANN spent a restless night, her mind in too much turmoil to be completely blanked out. Wild dreams tormented the few snatches of sleep she had. It was a relief to finally wake to daylight. Her thoughts instantly homed in on the man who was fast becoming the dominant factor in her existence.

Was he awake? Ann rolled over to look at the time. Six-thirty. Matt was an early riser. He was probably out at the pool, already having his morning swim. Ann was tempted to go for a walk . . . see him . . . but that would be out of pattern . . . possibly revealing. Better to wait for the normal course of events.

Matt had made no arrangement with her about breakfast. The awkward scene the night before had precluded any decisions being made on such mundane matters as eating. Ann decided he was sure to knock on her door at eight o'clock and simply expect her to be ready to accompany him.

She was ready and waiting, but the knock didn't come. By eight forty-five she miserably faced up to the fact that he did not intend to have breakfast with her. The convention was over. There was no reason for him to want her company. She rang room service.

No sooner had she put the telephone down than the knock she had been waiting for sounded loud and firm. Ann had to stop herself from racing to open the door. As it was, her pulse was racing faster with each slowly measured step she took. She dragged in a deep, calming breath before turning the knob.

He hadn't stayed near the door. He was at the table in the sitting-room, sifting through papers in his attaché case.

'Good morning,' Ann said stiffly, her voice tightening at the sight of him.

He was dressed in a light beige suit that contrasted attractively with his dark good looks. But his face looked grim when he looked up at her, and his gaze fastened straight on hers and did not waver.

'You know the limousine is calling at ten for the trip to the airport,' he stated briskly.

'Yes.'

'I've rung the porter to collect your luggage at a quarter to. I won't be coming with you. I have more business here.'

'But...' Ann floundered, torn by the need to stay with him, and the necessity for discretion where her own emotions were concerned '... if there's more business to do, won't you be wanting me?' she argued.

There was a dark fixedness in his eyes that denied any desire for her at all, and Ann felt a stab of despair even before he answered her. 'No,' he said curtly. 'You've done enough. Go on home. And take a couple of days off. It's been a long, hard week and you deserve a break. Wednesday will be soon enough for you to come into the office.'

There was no arguing with him. Ann could see that. She knew precisely what he was doing—putting distance between them, setting a cooling-off period that would reduce any awkward hangover from last night's 'madness'. Then back to business, pure and simple.

'Thank you. I'll do that,' she bit out, clenching her teeth against the wave of despair that was surging through her.

He nodded and looked down at his papers again.

Ann retreated into her room and shut the door. She packed her things with automatic efficiency. When her breakfast arrived she drank the freshly squeezed orange juice, forced herself to eat a croissant, and washed it down with coffee. The porter called for her luggage and she accompanied him to Reception. She didn't even think of throwing a coin into the pool below the waterfall. She left the Mirage Hotel in a limousine, just as she had arrived, except for one elemental difference. She was alone.

Fool, fool, fool, her mind chanted in an ever-echoing taunt. Matt had never given her any reason—not the slightest thread of hope—to think there could be a chance of him falling in love with her. He valued her head for business. That was all. That was all it would ever be with him.

On the whole, he despised women. He might want one occasionally, but, as he himself had admitted, it was basically to serve only one purpose.

She served another purpose—possibly more important than any other to his life—and he was not about to 'muddy his nest'. Whatever dark desires she had provoked in him from time to time would be ruthlessly contained from now on. That message had been written loud and clear on his grim visage this morning.

But desire was not love, anyway. She could have let him take her last night if desire was what she wanted from him. The situation had been explosive enough that the slightest bit of encouragement from her would have drawn him on.

As for caring about her feelings...he was almost certainly thinking more of his own...wanting a less prickly working relationship...winning her over with the pearl necklace...showing her he was a good guy to work for.

The situation was hopeless.

And to cling to a false hope was the worst kind of self-deception. To go on working for him, pretending he meant no more than a good boss to her, would only create another pattern of deceit. And he would despise her for it when he found out the truth. Which would undoubtedly slip out, sooner or later.

Love created its own need for expression. Her mother had taught Ann that. And the needs were many and varied. To clamp down on all of them was to stifle herself. Chantelle had never believed in stifling herself.

The thought jolted Ann into realising what she had been doing all these years, particularly since her mother's death—covering up, evading, denying or stinting those traits which had most characterised Chantelle.

The 'pattern of deceit'—Matt's words—and they were true in a much wider sense than he realised.

They haunted Ann all the way home, and she churned over them for the rest of the weekend.

She felt a squirming sense of shame every time she looked at her mother's photographs. Chantelle had never hidden anything. She had been open and honest and true to herself, no matter what anyone else thought of her. She had lived and died by her own lights, flouting convention, a brave, free spirit embarked on a never-ending adventure. And if one door closed . . . well, there was always another.

She had frequently made unwise decisions, but at least she had made them and carried them through. And not in any half-measures, either. No safe way . . . or cautious way . . . or deceptive way. And she would never—not for any reason—have hidden her relationship with her daughter, as Ann had done since her mother's death.

Love was not something that should be hidden. Love was a gift. It should be held out, shown, given, without any expectation of favours or guarantees. Whether it was taken or rejected was immaterial. It still enriched the donor.

Ann had made her decisions by Monday morning. They gave her a good, positive feeling—a more satisfying sense of purpose than she'd ever had in her life. She telephoned her mother's agent, who was only too delighted to hear from her, and eagerly settled on an appointment for Wednesday. She cleaned out her wardrobe, bundled up all her 'safe' clothes, including the three grey suits, and took them to a charity depot. She spent the rest of Monday and Tuesday shopping.

On Wednesday morning Ann rose earlier than usual. She washed her hair and blow-dried it into a fluffy, sophisticated bell-shape. Its shining fairness effected a classy style that would have done any shampoo advertisement proud.

She made up her face to complement the flamboyant outfit she had chosen to wear. Her contact lenses were tinted to highlight the blueness of her eyes. She lacquered her nails the same colour as her lipstick.

The dress was of a silky fabric that made the most of Ann's curvaceous figure. It had three-quarter sleeves and a long, dashing scarf that swung from the shoulders. But it was the colour that had the impact—kingfisher-blue and a rich, vibrant pink, mixed with an artistic flair that stamped it as a show-stopper. And the matching shoes and handbag heightened the effect.

Ann paused in the living-room before she set off to work, her gaze fastening on her favourite photograph.

'I love you, too, Mum,' she said softly. 'And you can be proud of me today. I've finally come to terms with myself and the world at large.'

People who passed her on her walk to the railway station turned to take a second look. A road-maintenance crew stopped work to stare. A wolf-whistle followed her. Angel Carmody smiled, enjoying the attention she drew. The crowd waiting on the platform parted for her. When the train pulled in, men stood back to let her enter the carriage first.

'Who is she?' she heard someone ask.

Amusement danced in Angel Carmody's eyes. Ann had travelled on this same morning train for years. But today...today she was unashamedly Chantelle's daughter, and everyone else could think what they liked.

When she alighted from the train at Wynyard Station, heads turned to follow her, and continued to do so all along the two city blocks she walked to her office building. Other company employees did a double-take when they saw her. Matt's receptionist, Sarah Dennis, shook her head in disbelief as Angel Carmody stepped out of the elevator on the top floor.

'Ann?' she said incredulously, her eyes dazedly taking in the woman who was not wearing a grey suit. Nothing like a grey suit.

'Hello, Sarah. Is Mr Fielding in?'

'Yes. But...' Again she shook her head, this time in sympathetic concern. 'I think you're asking for trouble.'

'Don't worry, Sarah. I've got everything under control,' Angel Carmody assured her.

Although a host of butterflies fluttered through her stomach as she opened the door into Matt's office, her resolution was not shaken.

He was at his desk, working through a file of papers. He did not look up. This was exactly how he had been when she had first laid eyes on him, yet there was a world of difference in how she viewed him now. It was both a pain and a pleasure to look at him.

She quietly closed the door and stepped further into the office before drawing his attention. 'Good morning, Matt,' she said—in her mind it was a salute of hail and farewell—and she said it with all the love in her heart.

His head jerked up, surprise and pleasure lightening his tautly concentrated expression. 'Good morn——' His bright return greeting died on his lips the moment her appearance stamped itself on his brain.

He half rose to his feet, then, in discomfited haste, sat down again. He frowned and fiddled with his papers, darting glances at her from under his lowered eyebrows. 'You...er...look very nice this morning,' he said, looking decidedly put out by the change in her appearance.

'Thank you. This is the real me, Matt. No more deceit. This is what I truly like to wear. And, from now on, I'm not going to repress my...' she smiled '...my rather wild and exotic tastes.'

A load seemed to lift from his mind. He relaxed and smiled back. 'Well, I'd have to say you'll probably be a traffic hazard, but it's fine by me.' His smile turned lop-sided. 'Distracting...but I'll learn to live with it. Just give me about ten minutes each morning to stop gawking at you.'

'You don't have to learn to live with it, Matt,' she said with a slight dash of irony. She opened her handbag as she walked up to his desk, withdrew the pearl choker he had given her, and her letter of resignation, and placed them in front of him.

His look of mild puzzlement was instantly replaced by a lightning flash of comprehension. His hand shot across the desk-top and clamped around her wrist. His eyes bored into hers in urgent enquiry. 'You said you'd stay.'

Her gaze dropped to the fingers curled so tightly around her flesh. Possession...domination...the will to get his own way whatever it took. But Ann knew it to be a trap now, and she would not be a prisoner to it.

'You're hurting me, Matt,' she said quietly.

He held on for several tense seconds before reluctantly releasing her wrist. 'I'm sorry,' he said gruffly. 'But you must listen to me.'

'It won't work,' she warned him.

'It will!' he insisted vehemently.

He banged his fist down on the desk-top and rose to his feet, instinctively using the power of his physical dominance to impress his will on hers. A shadow of distaste crossed his face, but it was followed by a settling of ruthless determination.

'I checked up on you with Bill Leyman,' he shot at her. 'I know you walked out of your last position because of sexual harassment. I can hardly credit that I was such a fool as to do what I did on Friday night, but I swear to you, I'm not such a fool as to repeat such a grievous error. You are safe from that kind of thing here. Safer than you'd be anywhere else in that...' he swallowed back whatever words had been on his tongue and waved an agitated hand '...if you want to wear those clothes.'

His gaze flickered away from her and he moved, swinging out from behind the desk and pacing over to the window before turning around to face her again. He lifted a hand to emphasise his points.

'There is no reason for you to resign. I stayed behind on Saturday in order to clean up that business with the Pearsons. And, I can assure you, there is no misunderstanding left as to the status of our relationship.'

His mouth thinned in grim satisfaction. 'In fact, I taught that interfering bitch a lesson she'll remember for a long, long time.'

The status of their relationship—the words were a strong reinforcement to the decision that had already been made. She felt a stab of sympathy for

Amanda Pearson—another victim of Matt's strong charisma.

'That wasn't necessary, Matt,' she murmured.

His eyes glittered at her. 'The hell it wasn't! Look what it's led to. And it's going to stop here and now! I will not accept your resignation. There's no reason for it and I——'

'Yes, there is,' she cut in firmly. 'And if you'll just listen to me for a few minutes, I'll explain why I can't keep on working for you.'

'Explain, then!' he snapped impatiently, his whole body tense as if he was waiting to repel an attack.

'You said something to me on Friday night...something that hit home very hard. You called it "the pattern of deceit"——'

'I understand about that,' he leapt in forcefully.

'No. Not all of it,' she retorted quickly, holding up a hand to halt his protest. 'You would have to have known my mother to understand. For a long time—even more so since she died—I've been re-acting against her life. In my heart I accepted and loved her. But in a narrow, judgemental way, my mind locked her out. As I've locked lots of people out. You, too, Matt.'

His eyes were watching her with absorbed interest now. She took a deep breath and continued.

'In denying my mother...and in denying you...I denied myself. And I thank you for bringing me to that realisation. My resignation has nothing to do with your mistake on Friday night. And I accept your word that it wouldn't happen again. But that's no longer relevant.'

'Then what is relevant? Why resign?' he burst out, his hands lifting in anxious need to grasp something solid that he could get his teeth into.

'I'm sorry, Matt. I know I'm letting you down by walking out without notice. But I'll let myself down even more if I stay.'

'Tell me what you want!' he cried, his eyes stabbing urgently at hers. 'I'll pay you more. You can work less hours. Just tell me what you want!'

'I'm going to pursue a professional career in singing,' she stated with simple directness, cutting straight through his offers.

Shock was quickly followed by fierce argument. 'You have a beautiful voice, I'll grant you that. But you've got a better head for business than most men, and you like it. You love it! I've seen your eyes sparkle with the challenge and the thrill of achievement. You can't deny it!'

'No. I wouldn't do that. And I won't deny how much I've enjoyed working with you, Matt,' she said quietly. 'But I can't work with you any more, so I intend to use the other talents I was born with.'

A conflict of uncertainties raged across his face. 'Why can't you work with me?' he pleaded hoarsely. 'I want you with me. I need you, Ann. I'll do anything to keep you.'

The admissions were torn from him, and for a moment they stopped Angel's heart, and hope blossomed through her mind. Until she remembered how attached Matt was to his own convenience. She sighed, but her eyes could not help searching his hopefully as she delivered the final line.

'You laid down the conditions when you hired me, Matt. And you were right. Not only for you, but for me. I can't keep working with you because I've done what you told me not to do—I've fallen in love with you.'

Shock and disbelief glazed his eyes, but there was no answering spark of love. 'You ... love ... me?' The words staggered from his lips.

She tried to cover the pain of her disappointment with a smile. 'It's not a crime, you know. And I'm afraid you can't order love. It just happens. But I won't worry you with it. I'm going. I'm leaving now. I have a star to follow, and I have the same will to win as you have, Matt. I'll get there.'

He just stared back at her, thunderstruck, a strange helplessness etched on his face.

She walked over to him, reached up, and pressed a loving kiss on his cheek. 'Goodbye, Matt. My best wishes always,' she said huskily, her voice caught in an ungovernable well of emotion.

His hands lifted and fumbled to her waist, but she easily broke away. She was already at the door when his voice cracked into compelling command.

'Hold it! Hold it right there!'

Ann's heart galloped in unreasonable hope, but her mind seized control. She turned and shot a lightly mocking look at the man who could not take being beaten. 'Lose gracefully, Matt. There's nothing you can say that will keep me here.'

'You can't just walk out after telling me that!' he argued, his eyes feverish with the need to cope with her declaration.

'Yes, I can,' she answered flatly. 'It's why I'm walking out, Matt. I'm saving you the trouble of firing me.'

'For heaven's sake! Wait a minute! I don't believe you. I don't believe what you're saying. You've never given me the slightest indication of that anywhere along the line!' His eyes flashed hot accusation at her. 'The absolute reverse, in fact!'

'What difference does it make?' she posed, the whole balance of her decision on edge as she waited for his reply.

His finger shook at her. 'You...are the most contrary damned woman I've ever met! And the difference is I want you. You've driven me mad with wanting you! And now...just when I'm firmly resolved that you don't want me, never will want me...you tell me that you love me. Which blows hell out of everything! You're just totally impossible!'

'So...I'm solving your problem by getting out of your way, Matt,' she stated evenly.

'No, you're not! There's only one solution.' He paused to take a deep breath, then in a firm, decisive voice, he said, 'We'll get married. That's what we have to do. We'll get married, then everything will sort itself out.'

It was her turn to stare at him, completely thunderstruck by his declaration. 'You...want to marry...me?'

'Yes,' he said, satisfaction lighting his face. 'That's precisely what I want.'

She desperately wanted to believe it was because he loved her, but she could not forget how he had described his marital requirements—a regular bedmate, someone to look after his laundry, shopping, and social life. Someone who didn't bore him.

'Why?' she asked, still clinging to hope. 'Because you fancy having me in your bed for a while?'

He frowned at her. 'I wouldn't marry anyone for that. I don't want you to walk out of my life, Ann. You're the only woman I've ever known who's capable of sharing it. And I value that. Very much.'

Every word carried the punch of truth. And she believed him. But he did not love her. He was thinking only of himself—his needs, his wants, his life.

Part of her wanted to give in, take what he offered and forget everything else. It could be a very satisfying life.

But she would not let the decision lie on such a convenience any more. Where love was concerned, it was all or nothing.

'I'm sorry, Matt,' she said with aching regret. 'I understand what you're saying. I hope you can understand me. I do love you, but I can't marry you. You want to use me . . . your way . . . and when I marry . . . if I marry . . . I want to be loved for all that I am, not just for what I can do for my husband.'

She forced herself to turn back to the door.

'No . . . No!' He moved so fast, he caught her arms before her hand reached the knob. 'I can't let you go. I won't let you go!' he rasped. 'Ann . . .'

Her heart thumped wildly at the need in his voice, but the need to be true to herself overruled it. 'Matt, from now on, my name is Angel. Angel Carmody. And half-measures aren't my style. You're strong enough to keep me here temporarily, but the answer will still be no.'

She stood completely still, caught in the tension of his decision.

'Why are you so intransigent?' His breathing sounded laboured. His fingers pressured, softened, pressured again, then finally slid away.

'You've been a thorn in my side ever since you came,' he said bitterly. 'I got on without you before, and I can do it again. So if you've got to go, then go. I don't care if I never see you again!'

Never . . . the word seemed to punch the breath out of her body and drain all strength from her legs. Never to see him . . . never to be with him . . . never to know what it might have been like . . .

Anguish writhed through her mind . . . he might come to love her if she married him . . . but if he never did . . . if he was only ever interested in himself and what she could do for him . . .

She turned.

Angry pride was stamped on his face.

Her eyes searched his again in a last desperate bid for a chance at happiness with him, but she saw no love in them, only bitter rejection.

'I'm sorry,' she whispered, her throat hurting—all of her hurting. 'I love you. But I couldn't live with you without your love, Matt.'

It was a harder thing to do than she had ever imagined, but somehow she forced herself to do it. She turned away, opened the door, put one leg in front of the other, step by step, and left him behind her.

CHAPTER ELEVEN

ANGEL closed her mind and heart to the regrets that would have savaged them. She plunged straight ahead with her plans. Her first step was to visit her mother's agent, who welcomed her with pleasure, and greeted her decision to pursue a career in singing with voluble enthusiasm.

However, personal enthusiasm was one thing— Chantelle had dragged her agent along to Angel's school concerts and he certainly appreciated her talent—but selling her voice to the general public was quite another thing. It would take considerable planning and appropriate promotion.

Of course, her relationship to Chantelle would open doors and win consideration, but Angel would still have to prove herself worthy of the promise her mother's name evoked. Angel was not about to leave a stone unturned to do precisely that. It was what her mother had wanted for her, planned for her, and she was determined now to fulfil that ambition.

After a long and mutually satisfying lunch, where all the career options open to her were discussed, and a number of purposeful decisions made, her new agent departed about his business and Angel proceeded to her next objective.

She revisited the dance studio where she had been
a pupil every Saturday morning of her school years,
and signed up for various classes. She bought a
video of the latest developments in modern dance,
went shopping for some leotards, bought a bunch
of fresh spring flowers, and finally made her way
home, determined to regard the future in a cheerful
and optimistic frame of mind.

If this door didn't open for her, she would find
another. Her mother had always said that life was
full of endless possibilities, and, if you couldn't try
them all, you should at least sift through a few.
Ann had only ever allowed herself small, safe
snatches of adventure in her clothes and the hol-
idays she had taken overseas, but she would give
her spirit free rein from now on.

She didn't want any more than a light snack for
dinner. She watched the news on television, had a
long, refreshing shower, then pulled on the new
black leotard and tied a scarlet sash around her
waist. She decided that physical action was probably
the best method of keeping thoughts of Matt at bay.
If she tired herself out she should go to sleep fairly
easily.

She pushed her living-room furniture back
against the wall to give her a clear space for practice,
then put the dance-tape in the video and switched
it on. Her muscles were just beginning to protest
against the strenuous work-out when the doorbell
rang. She turned down the volume, wondering if
she had been playing it too loudly for her neigh-

bours, then went to answer the summons, checking the safety-chain on the door before opening it.

Her heart leapt in surprise when she saw Matt Fielding through the limited space the chain allowed. But he looked so grim and purposeful that any pleasure was dimmed by the thought that he had come to pursue his argument with her. Whether the thought was transparent to him or not, he swiftly answered the question.

'I haven't come to repeat what I said this morning, Ann...Angel...' The harried look crossed his face, and the expressive brown eyes filled with urgent appeal. 'Please...may I come in? I'd like to talk to you.'

She forgot what she was wearing. All she could think of was how much she loved this man...and he had come to see her...talk to her...on a personal basis. She slid the chain off and opened the door wide.

He stared at her.

Heat raced around her veins. 'I was practising some dance-steps,' she explained. 'That's why...' Her hand came up to fiddle with the low neckline of her skin-tight leotard, her palm half covering one bra-less breast.

He stepped in and shut the door behind him, bringing a tension into the room that completely strangled any further words that Angel might have said. His eyes wrenched away from the detailed outline of her body and jaggedly sought some other focus for his attention. They fastened on the photographs of Chantelle.

'Your mother?'

'Yes,' she whispered.

He walked over to her favourite photograph, picked it up, his hands gripping the frame hard as he stared down at the beautiful face. 'You don't look much like her...except around the eyes,' he remarked tensely.

Ann tried to clear her throat. 'I take more after my father in looks.'

He nodded. He slowly replaced the photograph, taking his time in positioning it exactly where it had been. 'This question may seem immaterial to you. But it isn't to me....' He took a deep breath, then turned to face her, his eyes painfully probing hers. 'When did you know that you loved me?'

Why it was important to him, she didn't know, but she gave him the truth without any equivocation. 'It was after you left me on Friday night. Until then I was fighting the attraction you held for me. I didn't want to feel as I did with you. I thought...' She sighed. 'Anyway, I finally realised—after that dreadful scene—that I loved you. And there was nothing I could do about it.'

He nodded, accepting her explanation without question. 'I know the feeling,' he said in a quiet, strained voice. 'I once thought I loved a woman. We were going to be married. It was when I was just starting out, and I looked like losing everything. She backed out of the marriage. Failure wasn't her scene.'

Compassion twisted her heart as she realised that this was at the root of his cynicism about women. 'I'm sorry, Matt,' she said softly. 'That must have been very hurtful.'

'Yes. Yes, it was,' he agreed, but he spoke as if it didn't mean much to him any more. 'I steered clear of women for a while. Then, when I was successful, I found they came to me. Funny how it works, isn't it?'

He was grimly unamused.

'No. It's not funny, Matt.' Her mouth curved into an ironic smile. 'Believe it or not, you have more going for you than your wealth and position. Some of those women could have had genuine feelings for you.'

He shook his head. 'Not one of them would have walked away from me as you did. They would have grabbed a proposal of marriage as fast as I gave it, and counted the cost afterwards.'

He paused, and slowly added, 'I realised today...that I hadn't loved Janice at all. I didn't know what love was...until after you'd left me this morning.'

Her whole body tingled, as if it had been numb and it was springing to life again...beautiful, expectant life. Her pulse started to dance. Wild and wonderful music cavorted through her mind. Her eyes shone with the glorious dawning of new hope.

Yet there was a bleak, introspective look on Matt's face that stilled any impulsive move to go to him. He was not reaching out to her. He appeared to be struggling to come to terms with himself. So she waited, every nerve stretched with excited anticipation, every atom of her concentration on him, willing him to fulfil the promise of his words with the declaration she craved to hear.

His eyes searched hers uncertainly, a fearful appeal flickering in their turbulent darkness. His voice gravelled from his throat—forced, tight. 'I could...and did...cut Janice out of my life. More a matter of pride than anything else. She wasn't...necessary. I took satisfaction in doing without her.'

He took a deep breath. 'And it was pride that made me let you go this morning. But there was no satisfaction in it. No satisfaction in anything. All day...my work...goals...I couldn't think... didn't want to think. It was just...empty...without you there sharing with me. Any way I looked at the future...it was meaningless...without you in it.'

An anxious frown pleated his brow. 'But I don't mean...I'm not asking you to come back to work for me. And it's not that I only want to use you. I'll hire any number of people you like to do the things you don't want to do.'

'Then what do you want me for, Matt?' she prompted softly, her heart leaping in joyful bounds with every admission he made.

'I can change,' he asserted vehemently, and as he continued his argument his eyes raked hers with desperate intensity. 'It's only a matter of adapting to the possibilities. I do it all the time. You've seen the way I operate. You can't doubt that. And there's money to be made in entertainment. It can be good business.'

His hands stretched out to her, reinforcing the plea in his voice. 'You know we're about to buy into television. We'll take over a recording company, too. Invest in a theatre. Get into the entrepreneurial field. I could promote your singing career...share your life...work towards whatever you want to do...'

'Oh, Matt!' she cried in sheer ecstatic joy, and, driven by her own overwhelming need and love for him, she flew across the room and threw her arms around his neck. 'Say you love me! Say you do!'

His arms came around her, pressing her to him in a fiercely possessive embrace. 'I don't care who you are or what you are...as long as I can be with you,' he said, his voice shaking with passionate conviction. 'And no matter what you do, Angel Carmody, I love you. Do you understand that?'

'Yes,' she sang. 'It's very clear.'

'And I'm not trying to use you.'

'No. You're not.'

His chest expanded as he dragged in a deep breath. His eyes bored into hers, forcefully commanding. 'So you will marry me?'

'Yes, I will.'

A light shudder ran through him. 'You won't change your mind?'

'I promise I won't change my mind.'

'Your word of honour?'

'Absolutely.'

His sigh was one of shaky relief. He gave a choked little laugh. 'It's crazy. I've got you here in my arms, and I can't quite believe it.'

'Believe it,' she whispered, and to make assurance doubly sure she reached up to press her mouth to his.

Matt needed no further encouragement, but he did not kiss her as he had before. His lips moved lightly, sensuously over hers, tasting, savouring her response, then very slowly he deepened the kiss. His tongue played a tantalising dance on hers, exciting sensations that teased her into inviting more…and more…plunging quickly into an erotic intimacy that sent shafts of pleasure right through her body.

She opened her eyes in dazed wonderment when he withdrew. His eyes smouldered with the desire to please, to give endless pleasure. His hands ran down the curve of her spine, pressing her body into a pulsing awareness of his need.

'I want all of you,' he said huskily. 'Say you want me, too.'

'Yes,' she breathed, knowing it was right, knowing this was the time, and the place, and the man she could truly give herself to. 'I want all of you, too, Matt.'

She led him into her bedroom and they undressed, without haste, touching each other in a
gentle, exploratory way, taking an intense visual
pleasure in the gradual baring of their bodies.

'Not even in my fantasies did you look as beautiful as this,' he murmured, his eyes adoring every
line of her soft femininity.

'I had fantasies, too, Matt,' she confessed. 'I
wondered how it would be...if you held me...'

'Like this?'

He slowly moulded her body to his, soothing her
nervous tremors at the first full contact with his
nakedness with warm, caressing hands. She slid her
arms around his waist, hugging him tightly, loving
the feel of him, intensely excited by his strong
masculinity.

'Satisfied?' he whispered, rubbing his cheek over
her hair.

'Yes.'

He tilted her head back with soft, sensuous kisses
around her temples, then took her mouth with a
passionate hunger that sent all of her senses reeling.
Matt lifted her off her feet and laid her on the bed,
sliding down beside her, kissing and caressing her
in ways that sensitised every inch of her flesh,
sending shivers of pleasure all over her skin and
twisting her nerves into taut expectancy for more
and more sensation.

It was strange, but she found that she had no
inhibitions with him, and took a wanton delight in
touching him, thrilling at her power to excite and

give him pleasure. The smallest things gave her enormous satisfaction: winding the tight black curls on his chest around her fingers, kissing the pulse at the base of his throat, feeling the slight flinch of his muscles when she ran her hands down his back.

'Tell me what to do, Matt,' she pleaded. 'Tell me how to please you.'

'You please me just by being you,' he said, with such loving indulgence that she felt not the slightest inadequacy at her lack of experience.

And when he finally moved to take her she welcomed him with an ecstatic sigh, the aching need that he had aroused at last filled with a warm, heavy fullness that was right and perfect and so deeply, wonderfully satisfying that tears welled into her eyes.

It was amazingly easy to adapt to his rhythm...instinctive. She invited, encouraged each powerful thrust, incredulously feeling the muscles of her inner body convulsing around him, enclosing him, holding him, releasing him only in pulsing anticipation for the next exciting beat of his flesh mingling with hers.

Her legs curled around his taut thighs, owning him. Her hands stroked his back, inciting a deeper possession. Elation dizzied her as she felt the muscles straining through his body, heard the rasp of his breath, felt the tremor that heralded the peak of his need for her.

Wave after wave of intense sensation broke through her body, building to a crest of almost anguished expectancy. She heard herself cry out, and in the next instant felt the explosive release of his body mingling its warmth with hers, and the incredible splendour of that climactic union created ripples of intense pleasure that radiated through her entire being.

Matt wrapped her in his arms and rolled her on to her side, still locked to him. His chest was heaving against her breasts, his breath coming in laboured gasps. She stroked his back in blissful wonderment, hoping he felt the same incredible sense of fulfilment.

Slowly his hand lifted and caressed the fine silkiness of her hair. 'For the first time in my life . . . I don't feel alone,' he murmured.

Sheer undiluted happiness breathed into her deep sigh. He did feel the same. 'I'll always love you, Matt,' she said, with all the fervour of her heart. 'Whatever you are, whoever you are, and whatever you want to do, you can count on me loving you.'

He pulled her head back and kissed her with a slow sensuality that was deliciously pleasant in the aftermath of their passion for each other. Then he smiled at her, his eyes warm and darkly shining with his deep pleasure in her.

'They say that a woman sings better after lovemaking. I have a mind to endlessly improve your voice, my Angel.'

She laughed. 'I don't think I'll argue about that. But I don't want to burst into song right now. I just want to hold you and never let you go.'

He grinned. 'I don't think I'll argue about that. I figure I'm winning.'

'No, you're not. It's a dead heat.'

'More like live heat.'

She laughed again and hugged him tight, exulting in their certain commitment to each other. 'Are we going to fight all our lives?' she asked, snuggling into his shoulder and giving it a playful bite.

'No. But if you keep doing that, I'll have no trouble proving to you that this older man does not flag.'

'Oh, Matt!' She reached up and stroked his cheek in a sudden well of tenderness. 'You don't have anything to prove to me. Ever.'

He turned his head to kiss her palm. 'Neither do you, my darling girl. To me you are perfect in every way. I only wish we'd figured it out sooner. We've wasted over five weeks.'

'Think of all the tomorrows,' she said happily.

'Not while tonight is ours.'

He kissed her.

And she conceded his point without any argument at all.

They loved and talked and laughed together long into the night, revelling in an intimacy of hearts and minds and bodies that had been unthinkable only five weeks ago. Yet it was theirs now, and it was so incredibly precious that both of them knew that, whatever their differences, they would cherish the gift of their love for each other for the rest of their lives.

CHAPTER TWELVE

'ANGEL CARMODY . . .'

There was a roar of approval and expectation from the massed crowd.

Matt gave her shoulders a quick, reassuring hug. 'Lay them in the aisles!' he encouraged, his eyes shining with pride in her.

'There aren't any aisles,' she retorted with a nervous laugh.

He grinned. 'Do you never stop arguing with me? Isn't a husband supposed to be head of his house?' He gave her a little push. 'Go, wife! They're waiting for you.'

The compère had his arm stretched towards her. Angel walked out to centre stage, a slim figure in glittering blue. Matt had ordered the dress made especially for tonight's performance. The style was simplicity itself: high-necked, long-sleeved, and figure-hugging to her hips, but the skirt swirled to her feet in sun-ray bursts of bugle beads. Her appearance evoked another roar from the crowd. She smiled and waved and took the microphone.

She had sung in front of a small studio audience for television several times, and the record she had cut was selling incredibly well, but nothing had really prepared her for this. She looked out on a seemingly endless sea of faces and bobbing lights. It was Christmas Eve and the Domain Park in the centre of Sydney was filled to overflowing with people who had come out to enjoy the nationally televised open-air concert of 'Carols by Candlelight'.

A hush fell over the vast audience as the orchestra behind her struck the first chords of the song that Angel had been requested to sing. She thought of Matt, listening in the wings. She thought of her mother, who had swayed audiences just like this one with the expressive magic of her voice. She swallowed hard, took a deep breath, and the sound came . . . pure and true.

'Amazing grace . . .'

Not one voice from the thousands gathered before her joined hers in song, as they had in the previous carols. The whole crowd listened in silence until the last note died away. The applause began in a ripple and grew to a mighty roar. Shouts went up.

'Sing the "Ave . . ."'

'"Ave Maria"!'

A chant swept through the crowd, demanding the encore. Angel looked helplessly at the compère. The song had not been rehearsed with the orchestra. She had only been scheduled to do the one number.

'Sing it without music. You can do it,' Matt urged from the wings.

'Can you?' the compère asked.

She nodded.

He took the microphone. 'Ladies and gentlemen, and all you children out there...we must have quiet if Angel Carmody is to sing the "Ave Maria". This will truly be a solo, without orchestra.'

The crowd instantly settled down to a low buzz of happy anticipation. The compère handed the microphone back to Angel. For a moment tears swam into her eyes. It was a very special song to her. She hoped her mother was listening somewhere.

She sang straight from the heart, and it seemed that the hearts of everyone out there were lifting with her, singing in a silence so profound that it was almost like being in a cathedral.

Wave after wave of frenzied applause washed over her as she handed the microphone back to the compère, thanked the orchestra, and escaped back to Matt, who hugged her in ecstatic delight.

'You were beautiful! Perfect! They loved you. But not as much as I do,' he said with an ardent light in his eyes. 'Let's go home before I disgrace myself and make love to you right here.'

She laughed and gave him a quick kiss. 'Home it is.'

She and Matt drove up to Fernlea where his mother and his sister's family were waiting to celebrate with them. They had all watched the show on television, and Ellie's husband had champagne on ice all ready for them. In the spirit of the occasion, Angel was persuaded to accept a glass, with Matt archly promising that if she looked the least bit intoxicated he would whip her straight off to bed.

'You were definitely the star!' Ellie sparkled at her. 'I knew you would be. And your dress looked absolutely fantastic.'

'That credit is mine,' Matt said smugly. 'If I'd left it to Angel, she might have gone on stage looking like a bird of paradise.'

He was propped on the arm-rest of her chair, and she wrinkled her nose at him. He leaned over and kissed it. 'You look heavenly, anyway. Admit it.'

'You win this time,' she agreed.

He laughed.

'So what's next on the agenda?' Brian asked with interest. 'You two are so full of surprises, I can't keep up with you.'

'We've had something of a surprise ourselves,' Matt said, and grinned down at his wife. 'You tell them, Angel.'

She smiled, her inner delight shining from her eyes. 'We're going to have a baby.'

Matt's mother absolutely beamed with pleasure. 'Oh, my dear!' She was up from her chair in an instant, and hugging her new daughter-in-law with even more approval than she had showered on her at the wedding. 'I'm so happy for you. For you and Matt. You are happy about it, aren't you?' she bubbled.

'Well, it does force a temporary limit on Angel's career,' Matt commented drily.

'Don't listen to him,' she assured his mother. 'He's as pleased as Punch because I'm switching over to his business for a while.'

'Our business,' he corrected indulgently. 'It's all our business. And the baby is very specially our business.'

Ellie and Brian roundly congratulated them on their future parenthood, and good-humouredly warned them that life with children was a whole new ball game. They would be absolutely fascinated to see what Matt and Angel made of it.

'A success, of course,' Matt said with sublime confidence. 'Angel is perfect at everything else, so she'll make a perfect mother. And if I'm not a perfect father, she'll pull me into line like she always does.'

'I don't always,' she argued.

'That's when it suits you not to,' he retorted, his eyes teasing. 'And, right now, I'm drawing the line. It's been a long day for an expectant mother and I'm taking you to bed. So say goodnight to everyone, or I won't give you your Christmas present in the morning.'

'See how he threatens me?' she said laughingly as he pulled her to her feet.

They all exchanged goodnight kisses and happy Christmas greetings, then Matt tucked her arm around his and led her upstairs to the privacy of their room.

They made love with slow, sensuous pleasure until need evoked the passion that always drove them to an ecstatic joy in their marriage.

'Next Christmas we'll have a son or daughter to buy presents for,' she murmured blissfully, idly tugging at the curls on his chest.

'Mmm...If you're going to ask me what I bought you, I'm not telling.'

'I didn't ask.'

'I'm not going to spoil my surprise.'

'I didn't ask.'

'It stays a secret.'

'Matt, I didn't ask.'

'You always want to know everything.'

'I love you,' she whispered happily.

'So you ought,' he said, and nipped her ear.

'I bought you a fantastic outfit in sea-green.'

He groaned. 'I'll wear it in bed. Just for you.'

'You know, Matt, I've never seen you wear those underpants I bought you.'

He growled.

'I really don't like you having secrets from me, Matt.'

'I knew it!' He rolled her on to her back and kissed her very thoroughly. 'Now, go to sleep,' he commanded.

'I'm too excited.'

He sighed. 'It's a necklace thing with "spoiled" spelt out in diamonds.'

'Matt! That's outrageous!'

'Yes. It suits you,' he said smugly. 'Now, go to sleep.'

She laughed and snuggled down in the warm curve of his body.

Spoiled.

She was, too. Spoiled absolutely rotten with Matt's love. And she couldn't be happier! Life was beautiful. Love was beautiful. And most beautiful of all was the man she had married.

He gave her so much. Not just in presents. His time, his support, his faith in her. She hoped she gave him just as much. Then she remembered his joy in the baby, and rested content. Our special business together, she thought. The gift of love.

**In December,
let Harlequin warm your heart with the
AWARD OF EXCELLENCE title**

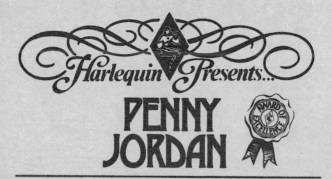

Harlequin Presents...

PENNY JORDAN

a rekindled passion

Over twenty years ago, Kate had a holiday
affair with Joss Bennett and found herself
pregnant as a result. Believing that Joss had
abandoned her to return to his wife and child,
Kate had her daughter and made no attempt
to track Joss down.

At her daughter's wedding, Kate suddenly
confronts the past in the shape of the
bridegroom's distant relative—Joss. He quickly
realises that Sophy must be his daughter and
wonders why Kate never contacted him.

Can love be rekindled after twenty years?
Be sure not to miss this AWARD OF EXCELLENCE
title, available wherever Harlequin books
are sold.

HP-KIND-1

You'll flip . . . your pages won't!
Read paperbacks *hands-free* with

Book Mate · I

The perfect "mate" for all your romance paperbacks

Traveling • Vacationing • At Work • In Bed • Studying • Cooking • Eating

Perfect size for all standard paperbacks, this wonderful invention makes reading a pure pleasure! Ingenious design holds paperback books OPEN and FLAT so even wind can't ruffle pages — leaves your hands free to do other things. Reinforced, wipe-clean vinyl-covered holder flexes to let you turn pages without undoing the strap . . . supports paperbacks so well, they have the strength of hardcovers!

Pages turn WITHOUT opening the strap

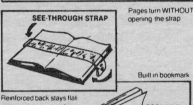

SEE-THROUGH STRAP

Reinforced back stays flat

Built in bookmark

BOOK MARK

BACK COVER HOLDING STRIP

10 x 7¼ opened
Snaps closed for easy carrying, too

Available now. Send your name, address, and zip code, along with a check or money order for just $5.95 + 75¢ for delivery (for a total of $6.70) payable to Reader Service to:

Reader Service
Bookmate Offer
3010 Walden Avenue
P.O. Box 1396
Buffalo, N.Y. 14269-1396

Offer not available in Canada
*New York residents add appropriate sales tax.

BM-GR

PASSPORT TO ROMANCE VACATION SWEEPSTAKES

OFFICIAL RULES

SWEEPSTAKES RULES AND REGULATIONS. NO PURCHASE NECESSARY.

HOW TO ENTER:

1. To enter, complete this official entry form and return with your invoice in the envelope provided, or print your name, address, telephone number and age on a plain piece of paper and mail to: Passport to Romance, P.O. Box #1397, Buffalo, N.Y. 14269-1397. No mechanically reproduced entries accepted.

2. All entries must be received by the Contest Closing Date, midnight, December 31, 1990 to be eligible.

3. Prizes: There will be ten (10) Grand Prizes awarded, each consisting of a choice of a trip for two people to: i) London, England (approximate retail value $5,050 U.S.); ii) England, Wales and Scotland (approximate retail value $6,400 U.S.); iii) Caribbean Cruise (approximate retail value $7,300 U.S.); iv) Hawaii (approximate retail value $ 9,550 U.S.); v) Greek Island Cruise in the Mediterranean (approximate retail value $12,250 U.S.); vi) France (approximate retail value $7,300 U.S.).

4. Any winner may choose to receive any trip or a cash alternative prize of $5,000.00 U.S. in lieu of the trip.

5. Odds of winning depend on number of entries received.

6. A random draw will be made by Nielsen Promotion Services, an independent judging organization on January 29, 1991, in Buffalo, N.Y, at 11:30 a.m. from all eligible entries received on or before the Contest Closing Date. Any Canadian entrants who are selected must correctly answer a time-limited, mathematical skill-testing question in order to win. Quebec residents may submit any litigation respecting the conduct and awarding of a prize in this contest to the Régie des loteries et courses du Quebec.

7. Full contest rules may be obtained by sending a stamped, self-addressed envelope to: "Passport to Romance Rules Request", P.O. Box 9998, Saint John, New Brunswick, E2L 4N4.

8. Payment of taxes other than air and hotel taxes is the sole responsibility of the winner.

9. Void where prohibited by law.

PASSPORT TO ROMANCE VACATION SWEEPSTAKES

OFFICIAL RULES

SWEEPSTAKES RULES AND REGULATIONS. NO PURCHASE NECESSARY.

HOW TO ENTER:

1. To enter, complete this official entry form and return with your invoice in the envelope provided, or print your name, address, telephone number and age on a plain piece of paper and mail to: Passport to Romance, P.O. Box #1397, Buffalo, N.Y. 14269-1397. No mechanically reproduced entries accepted.

2. All entries must be received by the Contest Closing Date, midnight, December 31, 1990 to be eligible.

3. Prizes: There will be ten (10) Grand Prizes awarded, each consisting of a choice of a trip for two people to: i) London, England (approximate retail value $5,050 U.S.); ii) England, Wales and Scotland (approximate retail value $6,400 U.S.); iii) Caribbean Cruise (approximate retail value $7,300 U.S.); iv) Hawaii (approximate retail value $ 9,550 U.S.); v) Greek Island Cruise in the Mediterranean (approximate retail value $12,250 U.S.); vi) France (approximate retail value $7,300 U.S.).

4. Any winner may choose to receive any trip or a cash alternative prize of $5,000.00 U.S. in lieu of the trip.

5. Odds of winning depend on number of entries received.

6. A random draw will be made by Nielsen Promotion Services, an independent judging organization on January 29, 1991, in Buffalo, N.Y., at 11:30 a.m. from all eligible entries received on or before the Contest Closing Date. Any Canadian entrants who are selected must correctly answer a time-limited, mathematical skill-testing question in order to win. Quebec residents may submit any litigation respecting the conduct and awarding of a prize in this contest to the Régie des loteries et courses du Quebec.

7. Full contest rules may be obtained by sending a stamped, self-addressed envelope to: "Passport to Romance Rules Request", P.O. Box 9998, Saint John, New Brunswick, E2L 4N4.

8. Payment of taxes other than air and hotel taxes is the sole responsibility of the winner.

9. Void where prohibited by law.

© 1990 HARLEQUIN ENTERPRISES LTD.   RLS-DIR

VACATION SWEEPSTAKES

Official Entry Form

Yes, enter me in the drawing for one of ten Vacations-for-Two! If I'm a winner, I'll get my choice of any of the six different destinations being offered — and I won't have to decide until after I'm notified!

Return entries with invoice in envelope provided along with Daily Travel Allowance Voucher. Each book in your shipment has two entry forms — and the more you enter, the better your chance of winning!

Name _____

Address _____ Apt. _____

City _____ State/Prov. _____ Zip/Postal Code _____

Daytime phone number _____
                          Area Code

☐ I am enclosing a Daily Travel
Allowance Voucher in the amount of $_____ Write in amount
                          revealed beneath scratch-off

© 1990 HARLEQUIN ENTERPRISES LTD.

VACATION SWEEPSTAKES

Official Entry Form

Yes, enter me in the drawing for one of ten Vacations-for-Two! If I'm a winner, I'll get my choice of any of the six different destinations being offered — and I won't have to decide until after I'm notified!

Return entries with invoice in envelope provided along with Daily Travel Allowance Voucher. Each book in your shipment has two entry forms — and the more you enter, the better your chance of winning!

Name _____

Address _____ Apt. _____

City _____ State/Prov. _____ Zip/Postal Code _____

Daytime phone number _____
                          Area Code

☐ I am enclosing a Daily Travel
Allowance Voucher in the amount of $_____ Write in amount
                          revealed beneath scratch-off

CPS-THREE